# THE ENGINEER

## MAGIC & STEAM: BOOK ONE

## C.S. POE

This is a work of fiction. Names, characters, places, and incidents either are the product of the author's imagination or are used fictitiously, and any resemblance to actual persons, living or dead, business establishments, events, or locales is entirely coincidental.

Published by Emporium Press
https://www.cspoe.com
contact@cspoe.com

Cover Art by Reese Dante
Cover content is for illustrative purposes only and any person depicted on the cover is a model.

Edited by Tricia Kristufek
Copyedited by Andrea Zimmerman
Proofread by Lyrical Lines

Published 2020.
Printed in the United States of America

Digital eBook ISBN: 978-1-952133-19-0

For Greg.
Now this steampunk is rightfully yours.

# I

The *trch*, *trch*, *trch* of Gatling gun rotating cylinders had been my only warning before the gunfire began. Bullets pierced the sun-bleached façade of the gambling hall behind me, and splintered wood rained down like an unexpected desert shower. I held on to my bowler, dove behind a nearby wagon, and scrambled up against the wheel. By way of defense, it offered little, but I desperately needed half a second to gather my bearings. I'd just entered Shallow Grave, Arizona, hadn't even flashed my badge yet, and already I was being shot at.

I yanked my traveling goggles over my head and accidently dropped them as another round of shooting began. Windows shattered, a woman's scream echoed from a few storefronts to my right, and the scorched red earth around me billowed up in miniature dust storms where bullets became embedded in the packed clay.

I lifted the headband and over-ear receivers of my Personal Discussion Device from my neck and fitted them into place. I raised the handheld transducer, punched in a code on the brass buttons that would connect me to my director back in New York City, and waited for Loren Moore's smooth tenor voice to answer.

But nothing happened.

I tried again.

Not even static.

"Send Gillian out West," I said in a self-mocking tone. I attempted contact a final time, but it was in vain. "Milo Ferguson won't stand a chance against him. *Of course not.* But the utter lack of basic amenities and technology?" More gunfire, and I winced before sliding down farther and trying to make myself as small a target as possible. "Gillian will *love it.*" I wrenched the band down to rest around my neck again, then rolled onto my belly to peer under the wagon.

There was a sudden crackle in the atmosphere—the snap of aether magic being activated. The sensation raised gooseflesh on my arms, and I recognized the spell for what it was.

Manufactured.

Illegal.

Not magic invoked by a caster like me, but by a physical weapon and someone with the wealth in which to afford its use.

And then three near-simultaneous shots fractured the air like seven years' bad luck. No doubt that had come from a triple-barrel Waterbury pistol. But it didn't line up with the intelligence the Bureau had on Milo Ferguson. Yes, he was wanted for his improper use of steam energy to power unregistered innovations, as well as his amassing of aether ammunition, but he hadn't once owned a Waterbury pistol or Jordan rifle, the only two weapons capable of firing magic-laden bullets.

Ferguson was an engineer. And mad though he might be, he was gifted at any sort of construction that had a lethal edge to it. His inventions were what had recently taken out half of Baltimore. His self-designed, magic-compatible monstrosities of brass and copper and iron were why I had been directed by the Bureau and the President of the United States to haul ass to Arizona territory.

So the shots in retaliation to the Gatling gun hadn't come from Ferguson. They'd come from yet another individual hell-bent on breaking the law. And me with only one pair of handcuffs and no idea where the town jail was located....

I watched from underneath the wagon as a pair of black-clad legs—presumably the Waterbury owner—ran by like the hounds from Hell were giving chase. The man skidded to an abrupt stop in the middle of the dirt road, turned, and another shiver of manufactured magic creeped along my arms seconds before the Waterbury shot another triple round at a target somewhere out of sight to my left.

I scrambled to my hands and knees and moved into a crouch. Peering around the edge of the wagon, I raised a hand to shield my eyes from the setting sun and saw, standing against a fiery desert backdrop, a cowboy straight out of a dime novel. He was tall, like he could steal the stars from the sky at night. Not a big man—lithe was the word—but imposing nonetheless in head-to-toe black attire, including a Stetson hat hanging from his neck. He remained in a shooting pose and cocked the hammer on his Waterbury. But as the ammunition came to life for a third time, gunfire erupted from my left again and sent the cowboy running for cover.

Specifically, my wagon.

He slid across the ground, sent up a cloud of dirt, and rolled out of the way as several bullets ricocheted off the hall. I'd stumbled backward at his approach and been knocked flat on my backside when he'd all but fallen on top of me to save his own skin.

He pointed the Waterbury at me, I revealed the federal badge pinned to my waistcoat, and we both spoke at the same time.

"You're under arrest," I directed.

"Who are you?" he demanded.

A beat.

The cowboy didn't break eye contact, didn't flinch, didn't seem to give a damn that I intended to read him his rights for gunfighting. But he did pull the black bandana down to reveal his face, and God save me, the man could have been divinity. Strong jawline, clean-shaven, surprisingly pale complexion, given the location, and blue, *blue* eyes that deserved a better, more beautiful adjective. Cobalt? Sapphire? Yes. His eyes glittered like dark gemstones.

Apollo himself would have taken inspiration from this man's face.

My throat was parched. I coughed a few times and managed, "Special Agent Gillian Hamilton with the Federal Bureau of—"

"Special Agent Hamilton," he interjected before beginning to rise, "I'm a little busy at the moment." For a man who'd just been shot at, his tone was frighteningly calm.

I grabbed at his coat sleeve and yanked. "Federal Bureau of Magic and Steam," I finished as if I hadn't been interrupted. "And you're under arrest for gunfighting and possession of an illegal magic firearm."

Before he had a chance to respond, a palm-sized brass ball, perfectly round and smooth, dropped onto the ground between us. It splintered open, stood on spiderlike appendages, and then the tiny inner mechanics began to spin and whir, the sound growing louder than what such a small object should have been able to produce.

"The hell is this?" I asked.

The cowboy ripped away from my distracted

hold. "Get up. *Now*."

His unease brought me to my feet without conscious thought.

"We need to go." He grabbed my arm, his strong blunt fingers digging into my clothing and flesh, and dragged me away from the inadequate safety of the wooden wagon.

I began to protest as the cowboy broke into a sprint that my much-shorter stature could hardly keep up with, but then I caught sight over my shoulder of what had managed to put the fear of God into him. That little brass oddity had grown to an impossible size, nearly the height of my own shoulders, and was ambling after us on its spider legs of spinning gears and steam-hissing joints. The top portion of the ball retracted back, and the ten-barrels of a Gatling gun unfolded from within. The cogs *tick*, *tick*, *tick*ed as it adjusted its trajectory and put us in its path of destruction.

"Christ Almighty," I swore.

I gave the stranger a shove and tore free from his grip. I raised an arm up and extended my fingers toward the sky. Thunder boomed from every corner of Shallow Grave and the air prickled and hummed with electricity as I tapped into the natural stream of magic encompassing Earth. When a caster—an individual with the ability to sense and utilize elemental magic—generated a spell, our bodies acted as a natural conduit. The raw magic passed through us without harm to our internal workings, while concurrently, our life energy replaced what was taken from the stream.

It wasn't a perfect relationship.

Years of spell casting built up a certain amount of magic refuse in our systems. It was dangerous for new or young casters to make physical contact with us veterans. The magic in our systems could shock, burn, or maim them in a dozen other grisly ways. Then there were the hazards of interacting with a caster who was our elemental opposite, and of course, it was *always* possible to overtax our bodies and temporarily lose the ability to cast.

Hell, as if there weren't enough safety considerations to living the life of an architect, scholar, or caster, it wasn't even a *legal* life until the Caster Regulation Act of 1865. Congress decided it was better—safer for the masses—to allow the practice of magic out in the open after its devastating uses during the Great Rebellion. Of course, bringing the magic community out of the shadows meant putting us under the strict guidance of the government.

Enter the Federal Bureau of Magic and Steam.

Mandatory documentation was the price I had to pay, but in return I'd been given a badge and a certain amount of respect that, as a boy, I'd never imagined possible. While I might have been under more scrutiny than most agents—the last thing the government wanted was someone of my skill level going rogue or losing all sense of their faculties—at least *this* aspect of my life was no longer considered shameful.

A bright bolt of lightning shot down from the sky and into my outstretched hand. The fractures of energy crackled, popped, and washed out Boot Spur Street in an illumination of a billion volts of natural power. I swung my arm around, looping the lightning like a lasso, then threw it with all my might at the Gatling spider.

It immediately exploded.

Metal screeched as it was torn apart.

Nuts and bolts, cogs and gears, whizzed through the air like miniature projectiles.

The Gatling ammunition detonated.

I waved at the smoke and unsettled dust in front of my face. The air cleared enough to show scorched black earth where the spider had stood. And it also appeared I'd set the wagon and gambling hall on fire.

*Shit.*

I winced as nearby voices cried for the fire brigade. I turned toward the cowboy, only to find him staring at me. He holstered the bulky Waterbury on his hip and said, "That's a clever little trick you have there, Hamilton."

A trick.

How rude.

And I had every intention of telling him so, but then another volley of gunfire interrupted. Farther down

Boot Spur Street, loping toward us at an unhurried pace, were two more Gatling spiders. These two had been the ones to initiate the fight with the fellow in black before he decided he had a higher probability of living if he were to run away.

The cowboy reached for me. "Come on!"

But I ignored him and raised my hand for a second time. I tamped down the intensity of the lightning—several million volts would be more than enough to obliterate the walking death machines terrorizing this mining town. Another arc of energy lit up the sky before it rushed to my outstretched hand the way ancient sailors of the sea crashed into rocks at the beckoning notes of a siren's song. I threw the lightning at the spiders and watched them burst in a similar, although admittedly less catastrophic, manner as the first.

Seemingly *done* with waiting, the cowboy grabbed my hand and squeezed tight. The warmth and roughness of this man's bare skin against my own, in a manner so brazenly intimate—he could have taken my wrist or arm, for God's sake—sent such a violent shock through me that it felt as if my own magic had momentarily betrayed me.

I don't touch anyone.

For one, I presented too much of a danger to others with magic in their blood. My skill level was not typical and, therefore, not well understood by the scholars in our community. Conditioning myself to remain clear of humanity as a whole was better—*safer*—for everyone. Although, to be honest, this was not the sole reason for my self-imposed isolation. Suspicion and rumor of my tendencies had circulated between the New York field office and metropolitan police force for years. Life was complicated enough as a caster. If it came to light that I, in fact, *did* crave the attention of men—mentally, emotionally, physically—I would be ruined.

So I pretended I didn't hear the whispers. Tempered the bitter jealousy churning in my gut when I witnessed moments of intimacy between others. And I behaved as if I didn't often cry myself to sleep due to loneliness.

"…before you set the whole town on fire," the cowboy was saying, bringing me back to the present. He set off in a run again.

This time, I followed.

We took a sharp right at the end of the block, turning onto Applejack Row. The sign was nailed haphazardly to a post on the corner, but as we sprinted past saloon after saloon, I realized the street had been aptly named. The gunfire had ceased after I'd taken out the spiders, commotion over the fire quieting as we put distance between us and Boot Spur Street, and yet the cowboy looked over his shoulder more than once—wary because we *weren't* being followed, it seemed.

He made a left turn onto a more populated

street. Business owners stood on porches, shielding their eyes from the setting sun as they looked in the general direction of where the sounds of danger had erupted. Groups of men, filthy from a day's hard labor in the outlying silver mines, hung together in small clusters around restaurant doors and at the cross street of Applejack Row. Only the boldest trotted to their watering hole of choice—cheap whiskey apparently worth the risk of being taken out by a stray bullet from those terrifying engineering marvels.

My—*the*—cowboy made another sharp left and ran down a narrow, dusty alley that separated a general store and two-story lodging. He came to a stop around the back, out of view from the curious and wary locals. The cowboy pounded twice, *loudly*, on the lodge door, all the while still gripping my hand in his.

I came to my senses at that point and said between taking in breaths of dry air, "Unhand me at once."

"Keep quiet, Agent Hamilton," he said with a touch of hostility. Despite this, I noted the man's speech had a certain refinement to it. Formal schooling, at least at one point in his life. His voice was deep— not booming, nothing so imposing. A low rumble, a little husky, commanding without trying to be, and it scratched an itch buried behind my heart.

The latch on the inside was released, the door opened a few inches, and a girl—no, a young woman—my height studied us through the crack. The cowboy's presence didn't appear to surprise or startle her. In fact, she immediately stepped back and allowed us to enter. I was dragged into a cramped, overheated kitchen. The cowboy didn't break momentum to speak with two older women, and likewise they didn't look up from the evening meals being prepared for lodgers.

Through another door, up a dark, single file staircase that would have creaked and groaned even under the steps of a ghost, then down a dimly lit hall that overlooked the front entrance of the lodge. The cowboy stopped outside the last door, pulled a large skeleton key from his suit coat pocket, and dragged me inside the rented room after him.

I hardly had more than a moment to take in my surroundings—a bed much too short for this looming cowboy now locking the door behind me, a squat table with a washbasin and clean linens, and a rickety-looking bureau too big for the room—all glowing gold as the last rays of sunlight shone through the far window. The cowboy moved around me with the fluid elegance of a cat, then in a single motion, backed me hard into the door, which knocked my bowler to the floor, and covered my mouth with one large hand before I could utter a word.

"Shh…." He stood close, body all heat and hard muscle that I couldn't ignore. I barely reached his shoulders. I was hardly bigger than most women, and this man was six feet of dominance towering over my slight frame. I wasn't yet thirty and my brown hair was mottled with premature gray, while his, unkempt by sand and wind, was as black as the wings of Nevermore. He was everything I wished I was and never would be.

The silence of the room was too loud.

The air too still.

The cowboy rested his forehead against the door, listening intently. His breathing had evened out after the run, and due to our proximity, it caressed the side of my face. It smelled clean, an almost herbal undertone with hints of sweet and bitter.

Chewing gum—Black Jack.

*Son of a*—How could I have been so dense? Allowed myself to be so preoccupied by his face, his body, the lingering notes of something woodsy mingled with fresh sweat, that I never connected the clues?

It was so obvious.

The Stetson. The Waterbury pistol. The licorice chewing gum he was rumored to love so much.

Not a cowboy.

An outlaw.

I shoved him back. *Hard.* "Gunner the Deadly."

He had a file with the Bureau due to his ownership of an unregistered magic weapon and frequent purchasing of highly illegal aether-laced bullets. But he was also the most wanted man in the United States. Every branch of law enforcement knew his record— over two-dozen counts of robbery, specifically of

Wells, Fargo & Co. airships. There were also the thirty-seven murders to consider. (Although I will be honest and note that *most* of his kills included known gangsters in big cities and cowboys bullying small settlements. But those facts did not make his decision to seek justice without consideration of the law acceptable.)

Rumor had it that Gunner the Deadly had never once been shot.

Had never been caught.

And here I was, standing two feet away from him in a locked room. I couldn't even calculate the odds of our predicament.

Gunner untied the bandana from around his neck and took a few steps to the window. He angled himself for a view of the route we'd taken down Applejack Row. "Your surprise tells me you aren't out West for me, Agent Hamilton."

"The latest reports put you in Tombstone."

"I left. Too many Earps for my liking."

"Too much law and order, you mean?"

Gunner turned around. His expression was there and gone, a flicker I couldn't read, and then he might as well have been raw marble an artist had yet to take a chisel to. "I know a powder keg situation when I see it."

I had nowhere to go, no immediate advantage for disarming and arresting Gunner with just *this much* distance between us, so I remained with my back against the locked door. "What are you doing in Shallow Grave?"

His face did that... *thing* again. Gunner's overall expression was so impassive. There was no hint of emotion around his mouth. No smile, no grimace, no nothing. But then I saw it. A minute narrowing of his eyes. Calculating. "Magic and Steam, you said?"

I pulled back my coat lapel and flashed the badge on my waistcoat a second time.

Gunner took a few steps forward, moved around the bed, which sagged in the middle, and took a seat on the edge of the mattress. He snapped the bandana in the air, releasing a small plume of dust. He set it beside him, yanked his goggles over his head, and put those aside as well. Gunner leaned forward, rested an elbow on his knee, and studied me with those dark, piercing blue eyes. "You federal sort don't come to the territories unless the situation is particularly grave. And it's not to arrest me, which I must admit, wounds me, Hamilton."

"My condolences."

He straightened and put both hands on his thighs. "Hmm... I know why." He jutted a thumb over his shoulder at the window. "A certain fellow... 'silver and steam and a little magic in between.'"

I recognized the quote. Newspapers all over the country had picked it up after witnesses to the explosions in Baltimore reported Milo Ferguson screaming the phrase to panicked crowds.

"Tinkerer," Gunner prompted.

"Milo Ferguson, yes. I'm here to arrest him."

"That's a shame, Hamilton." Gunner pulled a gold pocket watch from his waistcoat, studied the face briefly, then turned to look out the window again, his profile highlighted in the dying light.

I took the bait. "Why?"

"Because I'm here to kill him." So brutal. *Ruthless*. And said with all the calm and collected air of an educated man.

Gunner tucked the watch away and looked up. He wasn't a caster—he had no inherent magical talent, of that I was absolutely certain. If I shifted my perception and watched the tendrils of magic in the atmosphere, the glittering waves ebbed and flowed harmlessly around him. Magic wasn't attracted to him, didn't light him up like a steam-powered streetlamp that any caster with a strong enough skill level would be able to pick up on. He was like what the Bureau hired to partner with their magic agents, because it was too dangerous for casters to work together. A bruiser, we called them. Someone big, powerful, relying on body and smarts to crack a case.

And yet, for a man with no spells of his own, I felt an influence in the way he stared at me. I rolled my shoulders and pushed back against his nonmagic.

Gunner broke the enchantment, like he'd snuffed the light that drew the moth, by saying, "Those were Ferguson's—the Ten-Barrel Self-Propulsion

Arachnids."

"Rolls off the tongue."

"Indeed," he said rather dryly.

"So if they belong to Ferguson, why was the infamous Gunner the Deadly *running away*?"

The corner of Gunner's mouth twitched. He unhurriedly rose to his feet again, approached, and forced me to tilt my head back to keep eye contact. "I came for Ferguson, not his army of steam machines." Gunner unholstered his Waterbury.

I tensed, but all he did was show me the final round in the cylinders.

"I didn't have a lot of time to prepare," he explained, putting the weapon back. "When news of Baltimore reached Arizona, Ferguson was already in the territory."

"Airship travel," I confirmed.

"And of his own schematics," Gunner continued. "Fast and private. I took what ammo I'd purchased in Tombstone and came this way." He put a hand on his hip and struck a dramatic pose that I suspected was unintentional. "I should have had the element of surprise."

"Certainly didn't look to be the case."

Gunner stared at me. His eyes were so sharp it felt like his gaze sliced deep into my flesh, broke my ribs, and exposed the grotesque blackness I kept tucked inside. The idea that this criminal could see—*no*.

He couldn't. This was a tactical move. Intimidation, nothing more.

"Somehow he heard I was coming," Gunner explained after a beat. "I arrived this morning. These people are afraid. Ferguson is trying to take the surrounding silver mines."

I furrowed my brow. "He intends to mine the land himself?"

Gunner's expression didn't change, but with that narrowing of his eyes, the little wrinkles in the corners, I suddenly felt as if I was being laughed at. "He's testing its value in engineering."

"And so you've decided to take justice into your own hands," I concluded.

"We'll all be better off when Milo Ferguson is six feet under."

"That isn't for you to decide."

Gunner took another step forward. He was too close, overwhelming my senses with danger and heat and masculinity. "Should I instead leave this madman to a lone, unarmed special agent sent here from…." Gunner paused, and his eyes raked over me for clues as to where I called home. "A city boy, aren't you? Not Boston. New York. You're out of your element."

I squared my shoulders. "I don't need to carry a weapon, as you very well saw firsthand. And while we're on the topic of my aptitude, Mr.—*Gunner*—the President of the United—"

"Chose you? Yes, I'm quite impressed by your

curriculum vitae."

That pissed me off even more, and I felt my skin prickle like a storm was rolling in. "I know you don't find my person to be intimidating, but if you'll pardon my bluntness, I don't give a fuck. I have been an officer of the law for nearly a decade, and in that time, have apprehended some of the country's worst criminals. *Alive*, I might add."

Gunner smiled. It was startling to see such a sudden shift in his expression, and he wore the look well. "You haven't apprehended me."

"You're next."

A huff of air escaped Gunner, something close to but not quite a laugh. "Oh, I do like you, Hamilton." He put his hand on the door beside my head and leaned in. "Perhaps we can work out a deal. Something mutually beneficial."

*Is he mocking me?*

*Taunting me?*

*Or... does he?*

I swallowed hard, my Adam's apple bobbing painfully. My face felt hot and my palms grew clammy. "I don't—I'm not like that."

Gunner's expression glimmered, much like the snap and crackle of filament in the first steam-powered streetlamp installed on Millionaire's Row six years ago. Would it ignite?—did I misunderstand his suggestion? The red globe bursting into luminosity—realization dawning on Gunner's face. The glow of new technology—a light briefly shining inside me where no one was allowed to look.

But he said nothing of it. Instead, he lowered his head and whispered in my ear, "Let's take Ferguson down together."

I grabbed a fistful of his clothing with the intention of giving Gunner a good shake and shove, but I did neither. "Why in God's name would I join an outlaw?" Luckily, my voice didn't wobble.

"I've been working on my reputation for as long as you've been employed to undermine it," Gunner answered. "And I don't take kindly to having it steamrolled by the likes of Ferguson."

"Are you jealous?"

"A man who jerks himself off after blowing up innocent women and children has no right to be compared to my caliber of outlaw."

"Because you're such a gentleman," I spat.

Gunner didn't break eye contact as he said, "You're wrinkling my shirt."

I glanced at my balled fist and gently— awkwardly—released my hold.

Gunner took a step back and crossed his arms over his chest. "I'll admit this situation is bigger than what one man can handle. Will you do the same?"

My jaw ached, and I realized I was working diligently to grind my molars into oblivion. "He *does* seem prepared," I admitted at length. "But what you're suggesting… the enemy of my enemy is—"

"A temporary partner."

"Certainly not friends."

"Much too strong of a word," Gunner agreed.

"Aiding law enforcement in this one endeavor will not negate your status as a wanted man," I warned.

"Thank God."

"And you must realize that I cannot pretend I never saw you."

Gunner's expression was blank, and yet I could see enjoyment twinkle in his eyes, as if I'd presented him with the most exciting game of cat and mouse he'd played in years.

*What have I gotten myself into?*

# II

"You're a real copper, ain't you?"

I'd left Gunner to his own devices after agreeing to his business proposition—heaven help me when I tried to explain that decision to my director—gone downstairs, and paid for accommodations of my own. The woman who'd let us in through the kitchen door earlier deposited a meal of beef-and-potato stew along with a warm beer in front of me at a table pushed into a far corner of Bassett Lodge's front entrance. The strategic view allowed me to watch the front door and older gentleman manning the counter, who might have been the father or uncle to this young lady, as well as the staircase and overhead hallway.

"Do you have another sort around here?" I asked.

The pretty woman pursed her lips and gave a noncommittal shrug. She had blonde hair coiled high on her head. I recalled an article published in

*The Delineator* over the summer about simplicity in hairstyles these days and how the spiral bun was an uncomplicated affair that could double as a means to exaggerate the apparent height of a lady. I didn't find the women's monthly publication an exhilarating read, per se, but I did find women to be an enigma and quite difficult to interact with. The magazine at least provided me with a practical understanding so my daily exchanges were… tolerable for them.

"I'm a special agent." I leaned back in the chair and flashed my badge.

"With those magic folks?"

"That's right."

"Which are you?"

I spared the bowl of stew a glance. Wisps of steam rose from the chunks of browned meat and wedges of potato. My stomach rumbled in anticipation. I suppressed a sigh and asked, "What do you mean?"

"I read in the newspaper about those sort. Some use magic. Some don't."

"Ah. I use magic."

Her eyebrows rose. "May I see?"

"It's not a parlor trick, ma'am."

Her cheeks colored. "Of course. My apologies." She turned and walked away from the table.

I picked up my spoon and stirred the meal.

"Sir?" The young lady returned to stand over me again.

Putting the utensil down, I asked with considerable effort, "What is it?"

"Are you here to help Gunner stop Tinkerer?"

As if the man had a sense to know when he was being spoken about, the door to Gunner's room upstairs opened and he stepped out. We both watched him walk along the hallway and come down the stairs at a leisurely pace. He'd ditched the jacket and waistcoat and appeared far too comfortable in just braces and a loosened tie, with the sleeves of his shirt rolled back to expose forearms corded with muscle. Gunner spared a glance my way as he reached the ground floor, but that was it. He didn't break stride as he made for the front desk.

I didn't know what to make of that. Meanwhile, the woman ducked her head as he walked past us, another blush darkening her cheeks. The fact that we'd both been admiring Gunner's assets, and only her attention was welcomed, made me painfully uncomfortable by her company.

I wanted her to go.

To leave me alone.

The way it was supposed to be.

But despite myself, I asked, "You're not afraid of him?"

She raised her eyes, like she'd all but forgotten my presence. "Excuse me?"

"He's an outlaw."

"Yes, I know. But he—Gunner, that is—he's stayed in town before. Ain't never done nothing wrong. Keeps to himself, pays his bills, says *please* and *thank you* like his mama taught him."

Just behind her, the older gentleman at the front desk, with a mustache so bushy that I couldn't see his mouth, set a box of ammunition on the countertop. Gunner tugged his purple-tinted goggles on, picked up a bullet, and held it up toward the out-of-date gas lamps to examine in the illumination.

I directed my gaze to the lady once more. "He's committed many terrible acts, ma'am."

She fiddled with the sleeve of her dress for a moment. "Sometimes people have to do terrible things for the right reason, sir. World ain't never been black and white. Gray ain't so ugly a color."

I ate my meal after she departed a final time. Not because I had much of an appetite anymore, but because I knew I'd come to regret the decision in the middle of the night when my growling stomach woke me from a sound sleep. It'd been a long day, I kept telling myself. Airship food outside of first class left much to be desired, and then the unplanned shootout on Boot Spur Street had spiked my adrenaline in a way I'd not anticipated. I needed a hearty meal and a few hours of solid sleep in a bed that didn't rock with the motions of the sky, and I'd be ready to take on Milo Ferguson tomorrow.

Gray ain't so ugly a color.

No. I felt no sympathy for Gunner. At any time in his illustrious career, he could have approached the authorities and let us handle the criminals he'd taken out himself. There was nothing keeping him from the life of a concerned citizen. Gunner made very conscious decisions. He did not regret them.

That was black and white.

Gunner was still at the front desk. He'd asked a question, and Mustache solemnly shook his head. Gunner tried again, but the man seemed to double down on the bad news. Gunner tapped the polished wood with his strong, blunt fingertips, considering. Then he turned toward me.

Not a glance this time.

Not a once-over.

Gunner's stare could nail a man to the goddamn wall. I felt stripped down. Naked. Those blue eyes cracked me open, like how a fissure in the earth opens under enough pressure. His look once again shined light inside me, and I knew—*I just knew*—Gunner was able to decipher the coded script on my soul.

There was danger in my truth being read—understood—so easily by this man. A wanted outlaw. He could try to blackmail me. Use it as leverage against me. But in spite of that, there was a warmth in my gut, like alcohol on an empty stomach. I adored the look he freely gave me. The attention. The awareness. I'd gone to the Bowery once or twice in my life. Not for sex. Nothing like that. I'd gone simply to be noticed.

Noticed in the way *I* noticed other men.

And it'd felt so good.

It'd felt like how it did now—with Gunner watching me.

I hadn't realized the same of him earlier. After all, he was... everything I was not. A man like Gunner, so overtly masculine, so unequivocally dangerous— society didn't whisper about him. He was a known loner, but never had I read a law enforcement file that suggested he was a loner because his sort of companionship might *also* be found on the Bowery. But there was no other explanation for the way he stared at me just then.

Gunner shook Mustache's hand, collected the box of ammunition, and went upstairs.

As soon as Gunner's door shut, I stood, pushed the chair in, and approached the front desk. "Excuse me?"

Mustache looked down at me and then said, "Oh. Mr. Hamilton, was it?"

"Agent Hamilton, yes. Magic and Steam," I answered in clipped, concise sentences. "What did Mr.—Gunner—want?"

Mustache hesitated. He had droopy eyes. Droopy jowls. Like an old dog who'd been worked hard his whole life.

And he didn't want to turn Gunner in. Not for nothing.

*These people are mad.*

"I'm quite aware of his presence in town," I clarified. "But I'm here for Tinkerer, you understand? Mr. Gunner is not my concern."

*For now.*

This put Mustache at ease, at least enough to say, "He was looking to purchase some ammunition, sir. That's all."

"For his Waterbury?"

"I sold him a caliber that'll fit a Waterbury, sir. Ain't no aether in it, and that's the truth. Just regular bullets."

"But he inquired after a local caster? Someone to infuse the ammunition with aether?"

Mustache's jowls shuddered as he blew out a breath. "No casters in Shallow Grave. Present company excluded, sir."

"But he did ask," I pressed. Because of course Gunner would have. If one was going to own a Waterbury, one expected to use the correct ammunition.

"This here's a mining town," Mustache answered after a beat. "Nothing fancy. Hardworking families. But we don't welcome Tinkerer. We don't want to be another Baltimore."

"That's why I'm here," I answered.

"Aye, sir. But it's why he's here too. Gunner. And for as long as you're under our roof, I do hope you'll respect his decision to stick his neck out for a bunch of simple folks."

I took a stcp back from the counter, thanked him, and headed up the creaking staircase. I stopped outside my own door, fished free a skeleton key, and then hesitated. "Christ Almighty…." I stuffed the key back into my pocket, turned on one heel, and marched to the last door. I knocked loudly and waited.

"Come in, Hamilton," Gunner said, his voice still deep and smoky, if a bit muffled.

I turned the knob, gave the door a nudge, let it fall open, and stood to the right of the threshold. The room was awash in light from a gas lamp on the bureau, the window opened to dissipate the noxious smell, and there was Gunner, sitting in the middle of the mattress where it dipped. A toolkit was unrolled at his side, a box of ammunition leaning against his thigh, and he again wore goggles as he carefully tapped a hole into a bullet with the sharp point of some unfamiliar instrument.

"How did you know it was me?" I asked.

"Who else would it be?" he responded rather absently, not looking up from his work.

I took a step inside, shut the door, and said, "That pretty blonde."

"Alice."

"What?"

Gunner set the tool down, picked up a leather satchel no larger than his hand, and dipped his fingers inside. He sprinkled what looked like glittering sand from some faraway ocean beach into the hole he'd drilled. "Her name is Alice."

"It could have been Alice knocking."

"It wouldn't be Alice." Gunner stood, walked to the bureau, and leaned over the lamp to better examine the bullet.

I pressed my back against the door. "Why not?"

Gunner tugged his goggles down around his neck. If he was frustrated, that was the only indication.

"She's smitten," I continued.

"So are you." Gunner said that without bothering to look up. He walked back to the bed, sat, and loaded the bullet into his Waterbury. He cocked the hammer and pointed the pistol at the wall to his right, but there was no prickle in the air to suggest it had been altered with magic.

Instead, the energy causing the hairs on my arms to stand straight up had come from the simple honesty of Gunner's comment. Nothing more. "I—I am not—" My protest was cut short when Gunner turned his head and stared at me.

His face was still. Emotionless. *But those eyes.*

"Don't choke on your tongue, Hamilton. Men with our inclinations tend to recognize each other. No, don't panic. It's not one particular aspect about you. I just know. It's a survival skill, isn't it?" Gunner removed the bullet from his Waterbury. He didn't seem concerned about, well, anything.

Except the bullet.

How in God's name could he be so blasé about this?

"May I ask you a question?"

"You'll do as you please," Gunner said.

"How did you know I was from New York and not Boston?"

Gunner picked up the leather satchel and examined the contents a second time. "Your shoes."

I looked down.

"Richmond Bros. on Broadway," he continued. "They don't ship. You have to purchase in-house."

"So?"

Gunner glanced up and let out a breath. There was a suggestion of annoyance to it—in that way breathing could have a tone. "You don't strike me as a man who travels to New York to simply buy a pair of nice shoes. Ergo, you already live there." He stood, dropped the bag on the mattress, moved around the far side of the bed, and bent to rummage through something out of view on the floor.

I stepped forward and collected the bag of sand. I tested its weight in one palm, reached in to touch the contents, and as Gunner stood while putting a stick of Black Jack in his mouth, asked, "Are you trying to force magic?"

Gunner studied me from across the bed, his jaw working the gum.

"Because this is snake oil." I secured the drawstring and tossed the bag to him.

He caught it one-handed. "Worth a try, at least."

"What were you told that was? Aether-infused gunpowder? I suspect it's crushed geode."

He made a noncommittal sound.

"A registered caster could have told you that."

"I believe one just did." Gunner walked around the foot of the bed and stood before me.

I made an aggravated sound in the back of my throat and quickly yanked my suit coat off. I hung it on the doorknob before unbuttoning my shirt cuffs and setting them on the bureau.

"Don't let my presence keep you from getting comfortable," Gunner stated, crossing his arms over his chest.

I rolled my sleeves back. "You need aether bullets."

"I desire aether bullets," he corrected, standing completely still but watching my every move.

"They'll even the playing field, won't they? Against Ferguson?"

"Possibly."

"Then I'll infuse them." I finished with my sleeves and pointed a warning finger at Gunner. "But I want you to account for every shot. And any ammunition left unused after Ferguson has been apprehended must be returned to me."

Gunner's eyes did that minute narrowing again. He agreed to no such mandate as he sat on the mattress—the middle, to be specific—then patted the empty spot beside him. "Take a seat, Hamilton."

I sat, hyperaware of what little space there was between us. In fact, I was so close that I could smell soap on Gunner's skin—he must have cleaned up while I was at dinner—and the fresh licorice on his breath. I chose to focus on the faint stink produced by the gas lamp in the corner.

Gunner passed me the box of bullets.

I set it on my lap and asked, "May I borrow your goggles?"

"Your kept man didn't think to pack you a pair?" Gunner pulled his own over his head and handed them to me.

I swiped the offering and said woodenly, "I'm unattached." I put them on and added, "I dropped my pair earlier—during the shootout."

"I see."

Holding the box in my left palm, my right hand settled over the loose bullets inside, I performed a reverse-casting of aether.

It wasn't exactly easy.

Or legal, but that was neither here nor there at this point.

Aether was a bit like drawing on all of the elements in magic at once. It was a spell cast and utilized with magic still in its raw form. Absolute undiluted power—both healing and devastating. Aether was the lifeforce circling the planet. As a spell, it had no inherent weakness against other elements, which made it exceptionally useful in perilous situations against other casters, but it was also one of the most complex spells and obtainable only by experts. That was why aether-laced bullets were illegal and expensive— someone strong had to make them. Someone who'd either avoided the Caster Regulation Act altogether, or someone who'd gone rogue. Either way, it was generally bad news.

Reverse engineering aether was also different than simply using the magic for a spell. As far as our community was aware, aether was the only magic that could be manipulated in this unique way, which was also the only reason Gunner's Waterbury didn't have the capability of shooting something like lightning or fire bullets too. Instead of drawing on all of the different elements and letting loose a whirlwind of damage upon an opponent, I cast the spell on myself. Because I acted as a conduit when performing, and due to the healing force inherent in aether, no harm was caused to my person, and instead I felt full with a tingling, restless adrenaline.

After performing the spell several more times, I was so overstimulated that my hands began to glow an almost blinding white. Aether seeped from my fingertips like droplets of wine following the contours of its glass—down the bowl, along the stem, soaking into the tablecloth under the base. The excess had to go somewhere. And in this case, the magic, still unrefined and pulsating from contact with both the atmosphere and myself, leeched into the box of bullets. The light around my hands began to fade, then diminished entirely. I was left with juxtaposing sensations of physical exhaustion and an aroused mind. My stomach gave a sick lurch, but I managed to keep the beef stew down as I handed Gunner the ammunition.

"Clever trick," he said, accepting it.

"It's not a trick."

"No. I suppose it isn't."

I gave Gunner back his goggles and rose to my feet, and then the room took a sudden dip. I felt myself sway, watched the scrubbed floorboards come up to greet me, and heard the mattress give and the bullets ping as they fell. Then Gunner's arms were fastened around my waist, hauling me back into a standing position.

"Hamilton?" He loosened his grip, but my left knee buckled and he grabbed for me again. "All right... come, no, sit down. I'll fetch some brandy from the kitchen."

"I don't need brandy. Let go."

"Don't fight me. You nearly kissed the floor." Gunner forced me to sit on the edge of the mattress once more before crouching in front of me. He kept one hand wrapped firmly around my bicep. "What happened?"

"Aether infusion is illegal for a reason," I said. What was left of my stamina was going toward simply keeping my eyes open. It was such an odd sensation. I felt so spent that death wouldn't be a deep enough sleep, and yet my brain was trying to convince me I was quite capable of running nonstop all the way to the Pacific Ocean.

"What do you need?" Gunner asked.

"For you to stop manhandling me."

"I'm serious, Hamilton."

"So am I."

Gunner let go of my arm, swore quietly, and planted his hand in the middle of my chest when I fell forward. "Do you require a doctor?"

"No. It'll pass."

"Did you know this would happen?"

I dragged my gaze to meet Gunner's stoic expression. The room warped and distorted around him, like viewing the colored globes of streetlamps through a rain-streaked window. Or a photographer's attempt to catch lightning bugs on sheets of silver-plated copper. I laughed, but it sounded distant and unfamiliar. "It's something, isn't it? I'm a special agent."

"You are."

"And you're Gunner the Deadly."

He made a sound of acknowledgment.

"And right now, I'm completely at your mercy."

Gunner stood and leaned over me. He was gentle—hands stained with a history of blood and death, and the man was *gentle*—easing me onto my back. He patted my waistcoat, found my skeleton key, then left without a word.

I needed to focus on the magic in the room, the lodge, the town, the country. Allow its tendrils to carry me further and further until I was so twined with the elements that I couldn't tell where they began and I ended. Righting my enchanted footing, so to speak, would knock me out of this distortion. But every few seconds, I realized I was simply staring at the open planks of the ceiling. Counting the knots in the wood. So many of them.

The mattress made a sudden protest and lurched underneath me. For one terrifying moment, I imagined a hole opening and I was plummeting, *slowly*, into the nothingness, never to be seen again. Never to be lost to someone. Missed by someone.

Gunner's face appeared over me. It was his knee on the mattress and weight causing the dip that registered as a living nightmare. He got his arms underneath and hoisted me up in one fluid motion. He carried me out of his room and down the hall, and slipped into the open doorway of my own accommodations.

Floating.

Sinking.

Grasping for those arms again.

"No," I protested as sleep dragged me into familiar darkness.

My last memory of that night was a callused hand touching my face and a husky whisper near my ear. "Good night, Special Agent Hamilton."

# III

*October 11, 1881*

This was not my bed.

Not my home on the fourth floor of the bachelor hotel, The Buchanan.

Even the crisp bite in the air was not that of my city.

I had awoken suddenly. My gut lurched and my head pounded as if I'd spent the night with a bottle of cheap whiskey. Pour, shoot, slam the tumbler. Pour, shoot, slam the tumbler. Over and over until the intoxicating beat embedded itself in my brain. I sat up, gripped my temples, then took a brief look at my surroundings.

The bedside table had several items neatly laid out, perfectly aligned, as if their display mattered somehow. My PDD, which I'd tossed there the evening prior, before sitting down to dinner, had been straightened. Beside it were my shirt cuffs, pocket watch, key, and bowler. My suit and waistcoat were neatly folded on the foot of the bed. I leaned over the edge of the mattress. My shoes were tucked carefully out of the way.

My cheeks grew warm when a recollection roused itself. A whisper. A man's hand. That's right. I had been with Gunner the Deadly last night. I had, against my better judgment and the law itself, infused his ammunition with dangerous magic so as to give us the upper hand against Milo Ferguson.

The spell had thrown me for a spin afterward. And then… what? What had happened? I ended up here, in my quarters of this mediocre lodge that was probably as swanky as they came for a Wild West mining town. Had Gunner brought me to bed? Seen to my personal effects?

In God's name, *why*?

Why would he bother?

Why would he care?

Knuckles rasped the door, quick and quiet.

I pushed the blankets aside, got out of bed, and padded to the door in my stocking feet. When I opened it, there stood Gunner. He was dressed for the day—in all black, of course—with the Waterbury slung low on his hip. He leaned against the threshold, his face as impassive as ever.

"Good morning," Gunner stated.

"Oh. Yes. Good morning."

"How're you feeling?"

My face warmed again, hot enough to cook a can of beans on. "Fine."

He nodded a fraction. "Get dressed."

Something in those blue eyes alerted me, shook off the rest of my grogginess with a suddenness akin to having been dunked in a tub of ice water. "Has something happened?"

"Tinkerer was seen early this morning, stalking the perimeter of a silver mine called Big Mouth—about five miles outside of town."

I spared a quick glance over my shoulder. The sun hadn't even broken the horizon yet—the light still a soft and silky blue-gray. "Early this morning?" I repeated, looking at Gunner again.

He removed the pocket watch from his waistcoat and studied the face curiously. "Miners leave at about three."

"Christ."

"They sent a scrap of a boy back to report to me." He tucked the timepiece away.

"On horseback?"

"He ran." Gunner shifted and pushed himself off the doorframe. "*We'll* be on horseback, though. Meet me downstairs."

"Five minutes." I shut the door, undressed, and fetched my carpet bag. It'd been delivered by Bartholomew Industries, the airship company, after

I'd checked into Bassett Lodge and sent them notice. I removed fresh undergarments, shirt, and stockings, laid them on the bed beside the rest of my suit, then carried a leather satchel of toiletries to the pitcher and basin in the far corner of the room.

I poured water and dragged my fingertips along the ceramic bowl until steam danced across the water's surface, which was as much to test my magic connection as it was a desire to wash with hot water. The chill in the October air caused my bare skin to pebble with painful gooseflesh. With my nipples erect and balls drawn up, I didn't waste any more time in producing a bar of soap and clean washcloth. Afterward, I briefly examined my face in a small hand mirror. I could do with a shave, but there simply wasn't time.

I dressed, buttoned my collar and cuffs, tied my tie, and saw to a bit of Macassar oil in my hair and Crown Fougère on my person. Top notes of lavender and geranium, base notes of cedarwood and patchouli. A crisp, earthy scent that cost a pretty penny, but the gentleman at the boutique said it was sophisticated and suited me. He was merely trying to sell an expensive, London-based fragrance, of course, but the compliment had done something for my constantly battered ego. I'd been faithfully wearing it for a year now.

After slipping on my coat and grabbing my bowler, I headed downstairs. Gunner stood at a window near the front door, staring at the dim street through lace curtains while sipping what smelled like too-strongly-brewed coffee. He glanced sideways at me, then nearly did a double take.

"What?" I asked.

Gunner took a few steps and set the cup down on a nearby table. Then he walked to the door, saying under his breath, "Crown."

"Pardon?"

"You use Crown perfume." Gunner put his Stetson on and paused, his hand on the doorknob. "What is it? Not Buckingham. It's less soapy."

"Er—Fougère."

Gunner seemed satisfied by that response. He opened the door and took a step out onto the porch without another word.

I watched him from the threshold, slack-jawed. In the last twelve hours, the outlaw Gunner the Deadly was at odds with the man who I witnessed with my own two eyes. His current behavior did not nullify the fact that he was a vigilante at best, and a murderer at worst, but—*world ain't never been black and white*—I hadn't expected the gruff care he'd shown me last night. He'd unbuttoned my shoes, folded my coat, and tucked me into bed. I hadn't expected his frank openness regarding his own tendencies, like he'd meant to comfort me with the knowledge: I wasn't alone. And I certainly wasn't expecting the country's most wanted man to be familiar with and have apparent preferences regarding Crown perfumes.

Gunner was… complicated.

# IV

*October 11, 1881*

"Aye," a grisly middle-aged miner was saying as he chewed on the end of an unlit cigar. "Hamilton, you said?"

"Yes."

He nodded and combed his dirty fingers through his beard. "Aye," he repeated. "Tinkerer was here before daybreak. We knew he's been around these parts the last week." He motioned to the equally dirty younger men flanking either side of himself. "And the boys over at Fist and Nugget—that'd be copper and silver mines, respectively, sir—they seen him. He gave them a good scare too."

"Has he outright attacked any of the mines?" I asked.

The man squinted as he studied the horizon over my shoulder. "No, sir. Not exactly."

"Which means?"

The miner removed a dingy cap from his head and wiped his forehead. "Last week, Tinkerer tried to buy Nugget."

Gunner made a sound under his breath.

I shot him a quick look, but Gunner merely tugged the brim of his Stetson lower while his jaw worked a fresh stick of Black Jack gum.

"I guess that ain't quite right," the man continued. "He went 'round, started throwing double eagles at the lads, promising more where that came from if they handed over the daily loads of silver to him. You gotta understand, Mr. Hamilton—"

"Agent Hamilton," I corrected.

"What?"

I sighed a little. "Special Agent Hamilton."

"Oh. Aye. Er—" He chewed on that cigar some more. "Twenty dollars is over two weeks of work."

"Then the miners at Nugget have supplied Tinkerer with silver?" I concluded.

"No. They considered. We all did. Double the pay is mighty tempting. But he can't be trusted."

"We didn't take *one cent*," the man on the right piped up. His face was speckled with freckles, like an artist had flicked paint from his fingertips.

"Wise decision," I answered. "I'm sure it saved everyone's lives. Because I can guarantee that if Tinkerer got what he needed, he'd have destroyed the evidence afterward. If you understand my meaning."

The middle-age miner took the cigar from his mouth and pointed at Gunner with it. "That and because of Gunner."

"Pardon?"

"Ain't no one Tinkerer is afraid of. Except Gunner the Deadly. When he got into town yesterday, Tinkerer backed off. He's still testing our boundaries, but he's cautious. Less, ah… less *aggressive*. That's the word."

Was there not one person in Shallow Grave who didn't view this outlaw as a saint?

I pinched the bridge of my nose, squeezed my eyes shut, and said, "I appreciate your opinion—"

"It's *true*." The lanky third man finally spoke. "No disrespect, sir, but lawmen take bribes. They look the other way. They abuse power. Gunner don't."

On this point I couldn't disagree. I was from New York City. Our police force was corrupt beyond measure. It was only because of the Bureau's unique organization that we were protected from similar exploitations. Agents were compensated well, but the simple fact that we were all registered and overseen by the government made it difficult to accept kickbacks. Director Moore was also as honest a man as they came these days. He was constantly clashing with the police commissioner over city regulations and the harassment his agents were often dealt by coppers on the street.

The third man continued. "Just havin' Gunner in town keeps the gambling halls honest."

The freckled lad asked, "Wild Freddie—you heard of him, sir?"

I let out a held breath. "I'm familiar, yes. Cattle rustler, isn't he?"

"Aye. Piece of dirt tried to take advantage of my sister last year. She was fifteen. I was here—workin' the mines—otherwise you'd best believe I'd have taken care of him myself, sir. But Gunner stepped in."

I raised an eyebrow.

"Saved my baby sister's life and ran Wild Freddie out of town. He ain't never been seen around here again."

Lanky leaned forward to look around the man between them to ask, "Weren't he missing a testicle too?"

"When Gunner finished with him," Freckles agreed.

I spared Gunner a second glance and whispered, "You castrated a man?"

He didn't answer, but a flicker of what constituted a smile passed over Gunner's features.

Honestly, that was vigilante justice I could get behind.

"Thank you, gentlemen," I stated. "Before we go, would you be able to tell us where you believe Tinkerer has gone to?"

Freckles and Lanky looked at the older man for guidance.

He stuck the cigar between his teeth again and patted the pockets of his dirty waistcoat. "East," he grumbled.

"And what is in the east besides town?" I reached a hand out, snapped, and offered a small flame on the tip of my finger.

The miner jerked backward. His gaze darted between the magical offering and down at the cigar now clenched so hard between his teeth that he looked ready to bite through it. "N-no, thank you." He quickly took the cigar from his mouth and stuck it into a pocket.

I fought to keep my face neutral, lowering my hand and snuffing the flame out of existence. "East," I prompted once more.

"Dead Man's Canyon," the miner answered quickly, his interest in speaking with me so clearly over and done with. "The canyon is only 'bout a mile from town. Good a place as any to hunker down."

I turned to walk away from the men and general commotion surrounding the mine, but paused to watch Gunner reach into his trouser pocket, remove several silver coins, and disperse them between the three. Neither of us spoke as we mounted our horses—Gunner's a glossy-black Morgan stallion, mine a borrowed Saddlebred mare with a questionable disposition. Gunner took the lead until we'd put Big

Mouth at our backs, then slowed his horse to a trot and fell in alongside me.

"That upset you."

"What did?" I asked.

"His reaction to your magic."

"I'm quite used to it."

Gunner stared at me from under the brim of his Stetson. "It still bothered you."

I gave the reins a tug when the horse slowed to consider some shrubbery. "I don't enjoy being treated like I'm an oddity in a sideshow, no." I changed the subject. "You paid those men."

"I did."

"No one in this town seems to have a negative thing to say about you." I glanced at Gunner again. "Now it makes sense."

Gunner chuckled in an actual, honest-to-God, he-found-something-humorous sort of way. "Are you always so cynical, my dear Hamilton?"

I felt my face flush. "It wasn't cynicism."

"What do you think I do with the money I procure?" he countered.

*Procure.*

"I'm certain you'll enlighten me."

"I require very little in life. Black Jack, Folgers, and a loaded Waterbury," Gunner explained.

"Stetsons aren't what I would consider affordable."

Gunner put his thumb and forefinger on the brim of his hat. "Every man has an element of vanity."

I smiled. "So why appropriate the funds if you have no intention of keeping them?"

Gunner turned his attention to the trail ahead. He held the reins in one hand, his body moving in gentle sync to the Morgan's gait. He looked comfortable. Confident. Like a man who truly didn't need anything more than the hat on his head and the untamed wild before him.

"You said you've been working at the Bureau for nearly a decade," he began.

"Twelve years next April."

"In '65—when the government mandated casters come out of hiding and be regulated—what did you do?" Gunner gave me a sideways look. "Did you comply?"

"I fail to see the relation between these topics."

"It's a simple question, Hamilton. Did you, or did you not, comply with the government's order?"

I gave the mare's reins another jerk. "I didn't, no. Not right away. I was only thirteen."

"And yet I'm certain you'd lived a lifetime in those thirteen short years." Gunner's gaze didn't waver. "Enough to not blindly trust the promises of politicians in a war-weary country."

Conversations of this nature were setting me increasingly on edge. I couldn't understand how

Gunner the Deadly, of all damn men, was able to dissect and label the parts of me that no one—not even my director—had been able to successfully identify. And yet he managed with such ease and accuracy. Gunner was certainly an observant fellow, but God, was he a mind reader as well?

I sat up straighter in the saddle. "I made an informed decision when I reached eighteen. I had time to consider all of the implications—"

"Of letting someone know how powerful you are."

"Of the good I could do in return for the sacrifice of my privacy," I corrected.

Gunner nodded. "We aren't so different."

I snorted. "Excuse me?"

"I didn't wake one morning and decide to go out and break a few laws," Gunner explained. "I was put into situations that required making a decision. Not only for my well-being, but of those around me. I've never killed an innocent man and never stolen bread from the mouth of a child. Your files call me a vigilante, and if you must put a label to my actions, then yes, that is likely the most accurate. I've sacrificed my safety because I know I can do good. Sometimes bad men die when I do good. I don't regret that. I don't regret feeling alive."

"Alive?" That one word was so difficult to echo. Like it was foreign and my tongue could hardly comprehend the shape and structure of its syllables.

"I'll keep skirting the law and you'll keep enforcing

the law," Gunner continued. "But be certain your decision has allowed you to live. Otherwise, what's the point of taking a breath today if it does nothing for you tomorrow?" He was quiet for a moment before adding with a touch of thoughtful consideration, "I steal from airships because sometimes, I get bored."

# V

*October 11, 1881*

The sun had warmed the desert landscape by late morning, and I was sweating as we dismounted from the horses under the shade of a cluster of scraggly, weather-worn trees. I wrapped the reins over a low-hanging branch, retrieved a handkerchief from my pocket, and removed my hat to wipe my forehead.

"I thought we were going to a canyon?" I said.

Gunner inclined his head to the side as he opened a saddlebag and sorted through the contents. "Just over there."

I peered around him, squinting into the bright sunshine, but saw nothing other than shrubs and packed earth.

"Dead Man's is a slot canyon," Gunner explained. "It's a hell of a fall if you're not paying attention. We'll leave the horses here and climb down."

"Do you think Ferguson is actually in there?"

Gunner shrugged one shoulder. "This part of the canyon is the easiest to enter on foot. About a mile in, the passage opens into a cavern of sorts. Locals call it the Atrium. Good a place as any to remain out of sight while fiddling on whatever steam contraptions he's brought with him." He held out a parcel about the size of his palm, neatly folded in cloth.

I took it. "What's this?"

"You didn't eat before we left."

I opened the bundle to reveal dried strips of meat and hardtack. "Thank you." My stomach growled right on time, and I collected the beef in one hand before taking a big bite from all the strips.

Gunner waited, then took the cloth with the hardtack from me. He carefully refolded it, held it in one hand, and unholstered his Waterbury with the other.

"Unless that hardtack is from the war, shooting it seems excessive," I said around a second bite.

The corner of Gunner's mouth twitched, but he said nothing. He spun the pistol with quick, impressive accuracy, used the butt of the weapon to smash the tack, then holstered the Waterbury again. He unfolded the cloth to reveal the hard bread now broken into several smaller, more accessible bites.

"Clever little trick," I said lightly, accepting the handout a second time.

Gunner gave me a wink in response. It was such a

small gesture, as far as flirtations went, and yet it was so loud, so huge, it was akin to an airship exploding over the Lower East Side. My chest vibrated from the blast and my face was hot from the fire. Did Gunner look at every person that way? Strip them down to nothing but bone like a curious medical student, so he could understand how they were pieced together?

Or did he only look at men that way?

At *me*, that way?

Gunner reached out and my heart nearly stopped beating, because I was so certain he was going to touch my face. But he merely plucked a stray leaf from my collar. He tilted his head a bit, studying me again with those blue eyes, then said, "So much gray for a man not yet thirty. If I've done my math correctly."

I kept my hair cut quite close on the sides of my head where the worst of the gray was. But it was still obvious enough, at least to someone as perceptive as Gunner. "Mama's side of the family," I said after clearing my throat.

Gunner said nothing more. He took a piece of broken hardtack and put it in his mouth.

I finished the dried beef before saying, "The Bureau has estimated your age."

"Have they."

"Between thirty and thirty-five."

Gunner crunched the hardtack loudly, but made no indication as to whether that fact was in any way accurate.

"So?" I prodded.

"So what?"

"Are they correct?"

"I do enjoy that inquisitive expression you wear so often, Hamilton, but a man must keep his secrets from special agents. No matter how handsome they may be." With that, he turned and walked away.

Gunner was goddamn infuriating.

Infuriating and enigmatic and charming and— *lord save me.*

I popped two pieces of the bread in my mouth, shoved the remaining food back into Gunner's saddlebag, and hurried to catch up. I fell into step alongside him, both of us quiet but for the tread of boots on sand and rock for a dozen or so yards. I looked up at his profile briefly, which, of course, shared as much emotion as the smoothed surface of a river stone.

The Bureau knew little about him beyond his extensive list of crimes, but even some of those details were likely incorrect or hearsay. We didn't know where Gunner was from, and he had no detectable accent in which to make presumptions. We didn't know his age, although after careful consideration of the way he spoke and carried himself, and of the tiny suggestions of age around his eyes, I suspected he fell within our estimated age range. But beyond that, the Bureau and all other agencies of law knew nothing.

"Does anyone know your name?" I finally asked.

Gunner removed the package of Black Jack from his coat. "I suspect my mother had an inkling."

"No. I meant—"

"You meant, does a man know my name," Gunner corrected. He placed a stick of licorice gum on his tongue and returned the rapidly depleting package to his pocket. "I'm unattached, to borrow a phrase." He met my eyes. "I don't make it a habit to share such details with men who are nothing more than a passing ship in the night."

"Of course," I answered, a lightness in my tone that didn't match the sudden hurt in my gut.

Gunner put his hand out suddenly. "Mind yourself."

I directed my gaze down and immediately before us, only to realize the desert literally stopped here. The red-and-orange ground plunged straight down for nearly a hundred feet, much too steep and narrow to even consider climbing. The canyon itself wasn't terribly wide. I dared to imagine Gunner might have even been able to jump it with a good running start. It looked like a stitch had torn open in the earth.

"Well," I said after a beat. "Being magically inclined has its uses, but I'm not sure how *you* expect to get down there."

Gunner passed in front of me, dragging his hand lightly across my chest before turning and making a come-hither motion. He led the way toward a portion of the ground where juts of sandy rock protruded from the sheer walls, like broken teeth in the mouth of a boxer. Gunner started down the dangerous path first, moving from ledge to ledge like he'd done it a time or two. It was a slow and methodical process, but the temperature became noticeably more bearable as we neared the bottom and the sunlight had become diluted and less oppressive.

A few ragged rock outcroppings below me, Gunner's boot made a sudden scrape against dirt. The edge he stood on cracked and crumbled under his feet before he could grab ahold of any purchase. He didn't even get a curse out before he was falling the rest of the way.

I dropped to one knee, leaned over, and thrust a hand out. A strong wind erupted from the canyon's twisting pathways, screaming around the tight passages like tormented spirits. It kicked up sand, caught Gunner, and gently eased him to the ground. He raised his head and, for the first time, his face betrayed very real human emotions. I stood and jumped, a second gust of wind reaching like the hand of God was guiding me safely down.

Gunner had pulled the edge of his black bandana up to his mouth as the sand went every which way, only lowering it once I'd safely settled on the ground beside him. "Thank you," he said.

"You're welcome."

Gunner seemed like he had something else on his mind, even appeared to consider speaking the thought aloud, but he let that mask of impassiveness fall over his features again, checked his pocket watch, then led the way deeper into the canyon.

The trek wasn't as easy as I'd imagined—the passages at times so narrow we had to squeeze through sideways, or climb over boulders that had fallen into place when the earth had first split in two. But it *was* beautiful. The canyon was a burned-orange sandstone, a lovely contrast to the bright blue sky overhead. The lofty walls were smoothed and warped into fantastic shapes from Mother Nature's persnickety artistic vision finally coming to fruition after countless years of trial and error.

A fresh sweat had been worked up by the time Gunner came to an abrupt stop in a passage that had been slowly widening for the last several paces. He got down on one knee and retrieved something from the sand.

"What've you got?" I asked.

Gunner slowly rose, turned, and dumped a handful of loose cogs into my palm. I did not acknowledge the brush of his fingers against my own. He had done it purposefully. And while I did enjoy his attention very much, Gunner's subtle and authentic approach more impactful than anything I could have paid for at the Bowery, he had made the reality of his life perfectly clear—I would only be another passing ship in the night.

I could have kicked myself then, because I had

just, for however brief a moment, considered sleeping with Gunner the Deadly. And I had the audacity to be upset because we'd be nothing more than two strangers tossing each other off. The dry desert air must not have been good for my sensibilities.

"Hamilton?"

I took a breath and made a show of weighing the cogs in my hand. "There's a presence of aether in these. Very slight, but this material has been in close contact with aether ammunition for some time, I suspect." I tossed the cogs to the ground again and wiped my hands.

Gunner unholstered his Waterbury and cocked the pistol. He moved forward with slow, cautious steps, mindful of how footfalls echoed off the rock cliffs. He led us deeper into the canyon, and as we came around a bend, the passage suddenly opened into what I could only imagine was the Atrium.

There wasn't even a spare moment to take in our surroundings before the atmosphere crackled with living, produced magic. Aether ammunition. But not from Gunner's weapon. It came from farther inside the Atrium, and the magnitude was a dozen times more powerful than the Waterbury. I shouted Gunner's name in warning at the same instance as he turned and shoved me, and the two of us went sprawling to the ground. The aether explosion missed its intended targets and cracked the sandstone walls above us. Chunks of rock tore free and poured down like a fiery avalanche.

Gunner's long form tensed. Firm muscles and the hard angles of a male body pressed down on me, taking the beating from the falling debris. I knocked his hat off, wrapped my arms around his head, and forced Gunner's face into the crook of my neck and shoulder to protect what I could of him in return. Neither of us moved until the slip, slide, and rumble of sandstone subsided and a fine orange cloud of dust lingered in the air.

Gunner pulled back, breath sweet and warm against my face. He shifted enough to draw a hand up and wipe my cheek. "Are you okay?"

Was I? The well-being of my body was secondary to the very real and novel reality of having a man lying on top of me. I could smell Gunner's sweat and soap, and he too wore Crown perfume—its name momentarily lost to me. Top note of citrus, base note of a spicy, woodsy—*Sandringham*. That was it. And my God, even my most private, vivid daydreams did not compare to what it actually felt like to be touched this way.

My skin prickled and snapped and my muscles damn near convulsed. The sensations were quite similar to what happened when two casters touched each other. But there was no magic between me and Gunner, just flesh and bone and blood and heat and my heart *breaking* because the taste of human touch was confirmation that I wouldn't survive much longer in my self-induced isolation. I was wasting away inside, and Gunner was an antidote.

"Gillian?"

I startled at the sound of my first name on his lips, husky and a little raw. I returned my gaze to Gunner's but fell short of managing any response to his inquiry. His eyes were wild. His hand moved from my cheek to grasp my chin.

Gunner was going to kiss me.

And I'd allow it.

I'd allow this infuriating, complicated, law-breaking bastard, with a smile that made my knees buckle, kiss me—touch me—do whatever he wished with me. I'd welcome it. Revel in it.

Because for once.

Just once.

I wanted to be happy.

A maniacal laugh erupted from the Atrium, followed by the hiss and roar of a steam engine coming to life.

Gunner blinked, that light in his eyes—that hunger—gone. He swore under his breath, grabbed his hat, and stood. I scrambled to my feet, looked at Gunner as he put his Stetson on, and followed his line of sight. There, in the open space of the canyon, was a magnificent armored locomotive. It was wider than the trains that ran on New York City's elevated platforms. Bulkier. Steam poured from a vent in the back, and the ground under our feet rumbled. A long cylindrical tube stuck out from the face of the mechanical beast. I wasn't certain what it was used for, but I didn't like the look of it one bit.

Standing in front of the locomotive was a giant who could have shamed participants in a strong man competition. He had a bowler on and sported a fantastic curled mustache. He wore outrageous pinstripe trousers and only a buttoned waistcoat over his chest, laying bare his muscular and tattooed arms for the world to see.

Milo Ferguson.

He smiled a violent sort of smile and said, in an animated voice akin to a circus ringleader, "Howdy, Gunner. You're right on *time.*"

Gunner started to raise his Waterbury.

"Ah, ah, ah." Ferguson *tsk*ed while wagging a finger. He raised his other hand, outfitted in a mechanical fighting glove. It was similar to what street gangsters wore back home—cogs spinning and steam spitting as he flexed the jointed fingers. He pointed at me with the glove, and the cylindrical pipe on the locomotive mirrored the motion.

Manufactured aether kicked up and sent an uncomfortable static through the air.

Gunner hesitated.

"Remote-controlled aether ammunition," I murmured. I shot a glance over my shoulder and studied the severe damage the first shot did to the canyon wall. "A lot of it."

Ferguson tilted his head. He wore an almost comical, mad-as-a-hatter expression on his face.

"Who're you?"

"Special Agent Gillian Hamilton with the Federal Bureau of Magic and Steam." I pulled back the lapel of my coat to show my badge.

Ferguson rolled his head and bared his teeth at Gunner in another one of those bizarre smiles. He laughed and said, "Buggering a copper now?"

I bristled and called loudly, "By the authority vested in me by the President of the United States, I'm here to place you under arrest—"

Ferguson spoke over me like I was nobody. "You do *love* taking risks, don't you, Gunner? That's right. You always did. The more danger a prick presents, the more you want to fuck it. The more you want to taste it. *Choke on it*."

Gunner raised the Waterbury the rest of the way. "Stop." That was it. That was all he said. One word. No tone, no inflection, but the world might as well have ceased spinning at the command, if only for a moment.

Ferguson looked nonplussed. Then he grinned like a man possessed.

I cannot control time—scholars of the magic community do fear that such a spell might be possible with the correct caster and architect duo—but I did have the capability to take a mental step back. I was able to pick the moment apart, gauge the dangers, assess all possible outcomes, then act accordingly. It was, in a sense, like time slowed.

Gunner's finger was on the trigger of his pistol.

Ferguson's gloved hand released puffs of steam.

Gunner would shoot, of this I had no doubt.

But I instinctively knew Ferguson would first.

I held both hands palm down and then heaved upward, tapping into my magical connection with hard rock and dirt and earth to tear sandstone from the ground to use as a column of protection. Simultaneously Ferguson made a fist with his glove and the cylinder of the locomotive opened fire. Manufactured aether slammed into the rock, and it exploded in a shower of splinters.

Gunner moved seamlessly with how the seconds played out—his reflexes reinforcing why he'd "never been shot, never been caught." He stooped behind the sandstone, dropped to one knee at the release of aether, and turned his head away at the impact. Fluid and graceful, like a cat landing on their feet. He raised the Waterbury again and shot through the cloud of settling dust. His bullets hit the side of the locomotive, and I felt my magic reverberate through iron and... *silver*.

Ferguson's insane laughter echoed across the Atrium, followed by the slam of a metal door and locking mechanisms snapping into place. The locomotive lurched forward on heavily reinforced wheels, not unlike those of touring automobiles in design, and made directly for the towering cliffs. The top of the behemoth swiveled, and the cylinder fired another round of illegal magic.

Gunner took off in pursuit, leaving me to cover him. I raised one hand, palm upturned, then brought it down in a rush. A billion volts of electricity tore down from the sky and followed my motion, promptly colliding with the aether in an explosion of white and yellow light and a roar powerful enough to leave a ringing in my ears. The lightning bolt crushed the aether, followed the current to its source, and slammed into the locomotive. The machine staggered but kept rolling toward the sandstone walls and away from Gunner, who was giving chase. With a sudden screech of metal, four grappling arms—two on either side—unfolded from the locomotive, and the articulating claws buried themselves into the rock. And like some terrible mechanical monster, it began to scale the cliffs of the slot canyon.

The cylinder fired again, and again I let loose a storm of electricity. My magic was enough to overpower Ferguson's aether ammunition, but only just so. He wasn't shooting bullets like Gunner had in his Waterbury—the madman was shooting projectiles as big as shells used in field warfare. And with no inherent weakness in aether, the constant discharge from the locomotive was enough to keep me occupied while Ferguson successfully escaped.

The last shot from the cylinder was particularly volatile and ended up crushing my lightning spell. The charge snapped like a rubber band and engulfed my hands in sparks of wild energy interwoven with aether remnants. I swore loudly and shook my hands, the electricity dissipating as it fell to the ground. A few arcs bounced between my fingers, and the mixed-in aether drew beads of blood to the surface of my skin. I clenched my fists and gritted my teeth.

"Hamilton!" Gunner shouted, boots pounding the ground as he returned.

*Hamilton.* Not Gillian.

He skidded to a stop, holstering his weapon. "Are you okay?"

Blood seeped between my fingers and dripped down my knuckles. My hands shook a little as I relaxed them. "It's nothing. That last one got past me, is all."

Gunner didn't speak. But it was no matter. I felt I was beginning to understand those tells he had—the depth of his emotional state from the slight narrowing of his eyes, the words he chose not to voice that still managed to fill his silence.

"I'm fine," I insisted. "Let's go. We can't let him get away."

Quickly getting out of the canyon was a whole other matter. We didn't have engineering means, and I feared utilizing the elements would overtax me before we had a chance to take Ferguson down. So we ran. Back through the mile of twists and turns and tight crevasses before reaching the boxer teeth, climbing the precarious juts of rock, and safely returning to the surface.

The afternoon sun beat down overhead. My back and shoulders felt like I'd slept too close to an open flame, and I'd worked up a hell of a sweat that was overpowering the Fougère perfume. The horses whinnied and tossed their heads at our approach. It took a moment to calm them enough that we were able to climb onto the saddles, and after breaking into a gallop, I could see what had been the cause of their nervous state—the locomotive had come dangerously close and left tracks gouged in the baked earth.

"We have to get Ferguson out of the locomotive," Gunner called over the rush of wind and hooves. "Otherwise I'll spend all my ammo trying to put a dent in it."

"Keep those aether canisters off me and it won't be a problem," I answered loudly.

"That iron is too thick for lightning or aether magic to penetrate."

"It's the silver," I corrected.

"What?"

"Ferguson has already incorporated silver into his engineering," I called back. "It makes sense—the properties hold up well against aether." I looked at Gunner briefly. "Against *you*."

"But?"

I gripped the reins hard in one fist, raised my other, and cast a fire spell that danced in the palm of my hand. "He should be afraid of *me*."

# VI

*October 11, 1881*

Ferguson had made it back to Shallow Grave. He'd driven that steam-powered monstrosity right into town and now stood beside an open hatch on its left side in the middle of Boot Spur Street. In a booming voice, he demanded that the silver ore—packed and waiting for the lone evening airship that stopped in Benson to unload cargo due for the smelter before traveling to Tucson—be brought to him at once.

Before he did something... *regrettable.*

I pulled the horse's reins hard and swung down from the mare just as a clerk stepped out of an office with an overhead sign reading: Dexter Mining Co. "No," I said, so authoritatively that the poor man startled and spun toward me. "Give him nothing," I ordered, pointing at Ferguson a few storefronts away.

"But he'll kill—"

Gunner got down from his stallion, tugged his

bandana from his nose and mouth, and handed the horse's reins to the clerk. "Get these animals to the corral. And stay inside."

The clerk, visibly brightening at the sight of Gunner, nodded obediently. He took the reins of my horse as well, and with a *cluck* of his tongue, quickly led them away from the scene.

Gunner unholstered his Waterbury and cocked the pistol. "Work your clever tricks, Hamilton." He looked down, winked again, then took off in an all-out run, barreling toward Ferguson as fast as his long legs could take him.

Ferguson turned at the pounding of boots, ducked behind the open door of the locomotive, and easily missed eating three bullets. He laughed like a man truly unhinged, climbed back into his machine, and locked the door behind him. One of the mechanical arms untucked from the side and lunged at Gunner, its iron claws snapping like the beak of a bird of prey. Gunner shot again, this time blowing the claws to pieces, cogs and screws spewing in an arc across the afternoon sky. He dodged an attempt by the apparatus to simply bludgeon him with the smoking stump and then ran down a side street, vanishing from my line of sight.

Gunner missed on purpose.

The thought—a sudden realization buzzing around in my head like a gnat—had not spawned from nothing. Gunner the Deadly was a wanted man.

He was a deadeye marksman. He told me only the night before that he was in Shallow Grave with the sole intention of killing Milo Ferguson. So why, when his opportunity had been clean, had Gunner not pulled the trigger until Ferguson ducked for cover?

*Choke on it.*

Then it was like the gnat had been snatched out of the air and squashed between two fingers. The buzzing stopped.

*Gunner has a history with Ferguson.*

I had no tangible proof. No written accounts of such intimacies. Nothing conclusive I could point at and say, *Ah-ha!* It was only—Gunner had hesitated. More than once. Before meeting the man, I had thought that Gunner's skewed morality was based on the here and now, action and reaction, black and white. But if that were the case, Gunner would have fired true.

His past dogged him.

His past altered his expected response to a situation he had actively sought out.

His past grayed his thinking. Exposed Gunner to the vulnerabilities of man.

The curtain. A funeral pall. The Conqueror Worm.

The locomotive's axle spun hard, kicking up dirt as it turned to follow Gunner.

I shot after it, losing my bowler as I ran down the street and came up behind the locomotive. However it was that Ferguson viewed his surroundings from the inside, he apparently couldn't see behind, which was well and fine with me. I jumped onto one of the still-tucked-in mechanical arms, hoisted myself onto the fender over a massive wheel, and climbed across the locomotive until I was directly behind the top portion of machinery with the swiveling cylinder.

I pressed both palms firmly against the iron housing, closed my eyes, and sought out the silver I'd felt before that had been fused into the engineering. My hands turned red with the heat of a fire spell being activated.

The locals had said Ferguson feared no man but Gunner, and so he'd prepared his steam marvels accordingly—*orange*—to withstand the blasts of a Waterbury with illegal ammunition. Aether had no magical weakness—*yellow*—but certain natural elements could take the brunt of its power longer than others. And while agents at the Bureau were not typically on loan to locations outside of their assignment—*white*—there was a reason I was.

My spell found the silver, and it immediately began melting, leaving pockmarks in the structure. The mechanics glowed hot and bright, steam wafted, and sweat trickled down the sides of my face. I heard a muffled yelp from inside the locomotive, and then the cylinder fired an aether canister in the direction of Gunner. The kickback of the blast threw me right off the side of the locomotive. I hit the ground hard enough to knock the wind from my lungs, leaving me coughing and gasping as the side hatch opened and Ferguson scampered out of the smelter I'd created.

He turned, his chest heaving and eyes wide with shock. The ends of his impressive mustache were singed. He knocked the smoking bowler from his head and pointed a thick finger at me. "You little cocksucker." Then Ferguson lunged.

I sat up, scrambled backward, and rolled onto my hands and knees. But Ferguson grabbed the collar of my coat and slammed me to the ground again. My head cracked against a stone, my vision went white, and I tried to cry, but it came out more like a strangled breath. Ferguson wrapped his brass-and-copper-gloved hand around my throat and hauled me to my feet. He threw me up against the side of the locomotive. The fire spell didn't hurt, since it had been cast by me, but the heat was intolerable.

Ferguson tightened his grip on my neck, the cogs of his glove whirring and releasing steam. He lifted me off my feet, leaned in close, and growled, "Not even Gunner will recognize your whore face when I'm done with you." Ferguson tore the badge from my waistcoat with his free hand and tossed it carelessly over one shoulder.

I kicked wildly, held his massive forearm with one hand and punched at it with the other, tried to cast a spell—*any spell*—but I couldn't breathe, couldn't think.

"Let him go." Gunner slid into the edge of my

blurring vision, the barrels of the Waterbury pressed against the side of Ferguson's bald head.

Ferguson's hold loosened enough that I was able to gulp for air like a landed fish, but he still kept me pinned with my feet dangling. "Howdy, Gunner," he drawled, unfazed by the weapon.

"I said, let him go," Gunner repeated.

Ferguson tightened his grip again.

"I'll blow your brains out, Milo."

"No, you won't," Ferguson answered simply.

Gunner cocked the pistol.

Ferguson turned his head, allowing the Waterbury to slide across his temple and rest on the middle of his forehead. He grinned at Gunner, utterly wild.

I didn't wait to find out if Gunner was going to shoot this time. With Ferguson momentarily distracted and me seconds away from blacking out, I kicked him hard in the groin. So hard that Ferguson dropped to the ground like a sack of potatoes. I fell free from his grip, stumbled several feet away, and doubled over as I sucked in a deep lungful of hot air.

Gunner was at my side immediately, his hand on my back.

I nodded acknowledgment of his presence, my hands still on my knees and my eyes cast downward.

Gunner moved to stand in front of me, put a hand under my chin, and with just the slightest pressure of his thumb, encouraged me to stand straight. He tilted my chin to the side, tugged my collar down, and inspected my throat.

"Fine," I croaked out.

Gunner's hand moved to the back of my head next, and his fingers came back bloody. His eyes were like two sapphires on *fire*.

*Thud.*

*Thud. Thud. Thud.*

Gunner and I simultaneously looked down. Four brass balls cracked open and now-familiar spider appendages wiggled free. They rolled over, stood on their delicate mechanics, and began to double, triple, *quadruple* in size with every buzz and whir of cogs.

I raised my arm up, palm toward the sky to cast a lightning spell. The electricity weakly dropped down into my hold, sparked and sputtered, but I was unable to keep it alive and pulsating for more than a few seconds at a time. That blow to the back of my head left me feeling off-balance—as if I were lost in a cloud where two plus two equaled five, and I knew this wasn't correct, but I couldn't figure out the basic arithmetic on my fingers. My life energy was there. The magic was heavy in the atmosphere. But my scrambled brain couldn't…. I just needed a moment to correct my enchanted footing.

But we didn't have a minute to spare.

Gunner swore, raised his Waterbury, and fired twice—six bullets—into the nearest Gatling spider. It exploded in a mess of brass and copper parts before reaching its full size. He turned, took aim at a second, and pulled the trigger.

No manufactured aether buzzed along the surface of my skin.

No *crack* of a bullet pierced my ears.

I looked up at Gunner.

He clenched his jaw and lowered the weapon. "My last two rounds are at the lodge."

Ferguson started giggling. He raised his hands, four more brass balls held between his thumbs and first two fingers. "Oh, how the mighty have fallen, eh, Gunner?"

"This isn't the end, Milo."

Ferguson tossed the balls in between us, and they immediately hatched and started growing. "Time will tell."

Something flickered across Gunner's face at that statement. Too brief, as usual, but I was certain the realization he'd had was an important one.

Ferguson nodded his head toward me. "I'll give my condolences to the President, copper-pig." He laughed wildly, spun on one heel, and disappeared down Boot Spur Street.

Gunner glanced at one of the full-grown contraptions as its top opened with a hiss of steam and the ten-barreled Gatling gun lifted out. "I'm sorry you won't have that opportunity to arrest me in the future."

"I may forget to mention I ever saw you."

Gunner looked at me, an openly quizzical expression on his face.

The Gatling gun *tick*, *tick*, *tick*ed as it lined its sights on us.

I dropped to one knee, the impact sparking bright stars across my vision and making my head throb in time with my heart. "Keep us alive for thirty seconds and you've got my word."

Gunner spun the Waterbury still in his hand and ran at the closest spider. He smashed the butt of his weapon against the intricate mechanics over and over, steam and sparks shooting up from the backside.

I held one hand out toward the battered, melting locomotive, grasping onto the tendrils of fire magic within. I reached the other hand out and felt the faraway touch of water in the horse corral. I pulled my arms inward, pushing that magic into me.

Gunner holstered the Waterbury, swung around behind the spider as it lurched hard to one side, grabbed onto the base of the Gatling gun with both hands, and spun it toward the two other full-sized spiders as it opened fire.

I slammed my hands down into the packed dirt. My vision briefly shifted focus as I reconnected with earth magic. Wisps of natural energy ebbed and flowed with the breeze before snapping out of my physical range of sight.

Both spiders took the full assault of the Gatling

gun, one crumpling to a burning heap of garbage, the other's back legs collapsing, causing it to fire its rounds into the air. Gunner threw the spider in his hands to the ground, took his Waterbury again, and slammed the butt down on top of the other, forcing the barrels into the dirt, where they continued shooting. The spider's two front legs pushed back to dislodge itself from the ground, but Gunner moved around its backside, kicked it hard, and kept bringing the heel of his boot down until the gears and cogs were silent.

I held on to the essence of a spiral of air kicking up just outside the limits of town, rode that element into the sky, and reached for lightning again. Like a minute hand that'd been stuck at 11:59 finally jumping to midnight, my sight shifted to the magic plane again and I watched the different elements glitter and unfurl like fiddleheads.

Gunner's Stetson hung around his neck, no longer hiding his face. He looked incensed. Cheeks pink from exertion and eyes alight with fury. He was breathing hard as he finished with the three spiders in time for the next four to have grown large enough that the Gatling guns unloaded and started lining up their targets.

"Thirty seconds or not, you're out of time."

"Get down," I ordered, standing.

Gunner dropped to his belly without question.

I raised both hands to the sky. Thunder boomed overhead, and the reverberations shook storefront doors and windows. Black clouds formed, the streets of Shallow Grave darkened, and then two bolts of lightning came crashing into my outstretched arms. I brought my hands down and out to my sides, dispersing the magic across our immediate area. The four Gatling spiders immediately exploded. The lightning also slammed into the abandoned locomotive, frying the inner mechanics and rendering it utterly useless, even for an engineer as skilled as Ferguson.

I snapped and the lightning fizzled out of existence.

Gunner raised his head, looked at me, then sat on his knees to survey the street. "Goddamn, Hamilton." He got to his feet and dusted himself off. "At least you didn't set fire to anything this time."

He was impressed. I could hear a concealed smile in his tone. It made me feel feverish.

Gunner reached back to pull his Stetson on but paused when the locomotive began emitting a high-pitched *beep*. His eyes darted to the husk of hollowed iron, and then Gunner said quietly, "Come here."

"What?"

Gunner reached his hand out for me. "Now."

Confused but more keen to hold his hand than I was yesterday, I readily took it.

Without warning, Gunner burst into a sprint, hauling me with him. The beeping grew louder, despite the distance we put between us and the locomotive. We skidded around the corner of Applejack Row, and Gunner shoved me toward the back of a saloon. We crashed to the ground behind a pile of rotting sun-bleached barrels as a detonation from Boot Spur Street shook the ground.

I felt it was fairly safe to assume Ferguson had built and installed some kind of security device. Should he lose access to the locomotive, it would... self-implode. And my lightning had no doubt activated that trigger.

Whistles for the fire brigade sounded almost immediately.

Voices of citizens—shock, fear, surprise—filled the streets as they came out of hiding to inspect the damage.

Gunner's breathing was heavy against the side of my face.

I turned my head to look at him.

He slid a long leg between mine and took my chin. "Gillian."

This was it.

The moment I'd feared—*needed*—my entire life.

And to hell with the consequences.

*Just once, let me be happy.*

I grabbed the back of Gunner's head and pulled him down into a kiss. His mouth was strong, insistent, hungry for what it wanted. And I had no idea what I was doing. I felt clumsy and awkward in my attempt to keep up with his demand.

Gunner let up enough to whisper, "Open your

mouth."

"Wha—"

And then he dipped his tongue into my mouth. It was so obscene, so indecent, so brash of Gunner, yet I heard the sound that escaped me. It wasn't pain. It wasn't distress.

It was hunger. A thirst for more.

My entire body thrummed in a way I hadn't been able to imagine was even possible. This—Gunner's tongue twined with my own, sucking and caressing, dominant and masculine—this had to be why, once experienced, men with our inclinations were willing to brave any danger to feel this desire again.

This *want* again.

*Rightness* again.

Although pinned underneath him, I snaked my hands between us enough to attempt pushing Gunner's coat from his shoulders. I didn't get very far and instead loosened his tie with a firm tug.

Gunner grunted and broke the kiss. He stared at me for a beat, put his hand over mine, and pulled his tie free from my hold in order to sit up. "Not here." He grabbed his hat and got to his feet in a quick, seamless movement before reaching out to me.

I was not as graceful as I stood. "Where are we going?"

"Bassett Lodge." He moved around me, taking a shortcut through the back properties of shops along

Applejack Row.

"What about Ferguson's locomotive?" I asked, following close on Gunner's heel.

He looked over his shoulder but didn't stop walking. "I don't think it's going anywhere. Do you?"

"Well, no—"

"Then don't worry about it."

I opened my mouth to protest further. We couldn't leave the site as-is. We ought to return and oversee the situation. But the objections were halfhearted at best and never made it past the flutter of terrified excitement in my throat.

Upon reaching the back entrance of the lodge, Gunner knocked on the door as he had done yesterday.

I watched a bead of sweat roll down the contour of his jaw and disappear underneath the collar of his shirt. I wanted to follow that line of perspiration with my hands and mouth, divest Gunner of his renowned black wardrobe, and experience the body underneath in the same wicked ways as men before me had. I prayed this moment of intimacy we were to share would sate my starvation for years to come.

Because Gunner had been clear about how he handled sexual encounters.

Because he was an outlaw and I was a federal agent.

Because men like us did not have the possibility of… anything more.

Gunner looked down at me just then. Those blue eyes met mine, a smile ghosted across his face, and my heart panged with a profound longing to know his real name.

The door unlocked from the inside, Alice peered through the crack, then she immediately moved aside. She had a blush on her face as Gunner stepped past her and into the kitchen. No doubt the sight and smell of masculine physical exertion affected her as it did me.

I followed him inside, inclined my head to Alice in thanks, and trailed behind Gunner through the next door that exited the kitchen. He led the way single file up the stairs that, despite the afternoon light from the front windows, was still shrouded in relative darkness. The only indication of our ascent was the creak and groan of weathered floorboards underfoot.

Gunner removed a key from his inner coat pocket, unlocked the last door, hooked a finger under my collar, and tugged me inside. He shut the door, then shoved me back against it. He loomed over me, all heat and hard planes, dangerous as sure as the sun was to rise each morning, but unlike yesterday, I didn't push him away.

I grabbed Gunner's slender hips, yanked him closer, and pressed our bodies together. He threw his hat somewhere over his shoulder before leaning down to kiss me. He shrugged out of his coat at the same time, letting it fall to the floor, and brought his hands up to hold my face as he pushed his tongue between my lips. My hands fumbled as I again tasted the tang of licorice while Gunner's thumbs caressed my cheekbones. A few more of those kisses and I'd spend like an adolescent boy with no control.

With renewed desire to not let this end before it began, I broke from Gunner's kiss in order to look down and work the buttons of his trousers. He made a sound in the back of his throat—approval, that much I knew—and hastily unbuttoned his waistcoat. It dropped to the floor with a *thud*—the pocket watch, I suspected. Gunner pushed the braces from his shoulders, made short work of his tie, collar, cuffs, bandana, and goggles, then shoved my own suit coat off as soon as I'd finished with his trousers.

"You've much too many layers on, Hamilton."

"Gillian," I corrected.

Gunner smiled. It wasn't big and wide, nothing so bold for a man as subtle as himself, but it was still genuine. Enough to make my heart trip a few beats. "Gillian," he repeated in that low voice of his. "Finish up."

He pulled his boots off, turned, and walked to the foot of the bed, where he looped his holster around the railing before dropping his trousers and shirt to the floor. I tried not to gape at the openness in which Gunner disrobed, his casualness in removing vest and drawers, like he enjoyed his audience of one. And when his pale body was finally exposed, naked and handsome, backlit by the afternoon sun, my mouth had gone completely dry.

Gunner had black chest hair and a fine line that traveled from his navel to the groomed bush around his erect prick. His thighs and calves, much like his forearms, had fine, soft-looking black hairs. He bent down to rummage in what sounded like a carpet bag on the floor just out of sight, then straightened with a tin in one hand.

"Your unwavering interest is appreciated," Gunner began, looking at me as he popped the lid off. "But I had thought to use more than eyes."

I blinked, looked down at my state of partial undress, and felt a blush creep up my neck and cheeks. "Yes, of course. Sorry."

I made it a point to not look at Gunner again as I undressed. My own manner was methodical. Nothing so natural as how he had shed his garments. I wasn't sensual. I couldn't have been. I was so... *God.* I had no idea what I was doing.

I cast my undergarments to the floor and stared at myself. Not nearly as toned as Gunner. I touched my chest and thought, *Less hair too.* In fact, if I was correct that Gunner had a past with Ferguson—a man who'd proven he could squash me with his bare hands given the opportunity—why the hell was Gunner even interested?

"Gillian?"

I jerked my head up.

Gunner sat on the far edge of the bed. "Come lie

down."

I felt automated as I moved forward, awkwardly sat, then scooted back enough to lie as instructed. Belly-up was the ultimate act of submission, wasn't it?

Gunner rolled onto his side and draped his body over mine. The shock of bare skin on skin was immediate. I think I cried out, because Gunner was shushing and kissing me. My replication of his earlier ministrations wasn't perfect nor seamless, but I tried. I grabbed a handful of his gorgeous black hair, gave it a tug, and tentatively slid my tongue between his parted lips. Gunner eagerly opened to it. He thrust his hips lightly against my leg, drawing his hard prick up and down my thigh.

He broke the kiss, took a deep breath as if he'd been running for miles, and whispered against my ear, "Raise your leg. Knee to chest—that's it."

Was Gunner providing directions because he simply found me too slow for the upkeep of his own interests, or had he realized my earlier deflections, my *unattachment*—it was because I was a virgin? That I hadn't even been kissed, so *of course* I'd needed that explained too? My spiral of self-loathing was halted abruptly when Gunner moved his hand to my backside and pressed a slick, cool finger in my hole. I jumped and scooted back from the invasion.

"Sorry," Gunner said, raising his hand, and now I could see—that tin had had Vaseline in it. "Did I hurt you?"

I'd wanted to say *no*. It hadn't hurt me. Only surprised me. Wanted to say that I'd craved this my entire adult life—to experience for myself what the underground pamphlets described with words like: delicious, heavenly, fullness. That I just *knew* I needed it like I needed air in my lungs.

But I didn't tell Gunner any of that. I was in a bed, naked, with a man who should have existed only in fantasies, and I hadn't the courage to follow through on what was likely my only chance at sex before death.

"I'm not... sure."

"That I hurt you?"

"About doing this," I corrected.

Nothing on Gunner's face had changed, but I was struck by the notion that he was suddenly disappointed. For some reason, that touched me. Brought my defenses down.

"It's because I'm a virgin," I blurted out.

And then a sort of softness took over Gunner's features. He leaned down and kissed my mouth again. "We all are at one point, Gillian."

"I know that."

Gunner rested his slick hand just above my prick, stroking my skin lightly. He rubbed the tip of his nose against mine and said, "Another time."

Another time?

Had Gunner meant to imply—what, exactly? He would delight falling into bed with me again? That I wasn't a nameless ship sailing through his night? Or were these merely those good manners of his?

Gunner tilted his head and started kissing along my jaw. "We can do something else."

"We can?"

He murmured an agreement against my skin, moved his slippery hand down, and wrapped it around my length. Gunner stroked a few times and asked, "Okay?"

Was he kidding? *Okay?*

It was nothing like when I did it to myself. A different angle, stronger grip, callused touch—it was perfect, plain and simple.

"Y-yes," I gasped.

"On your side," Gunner instructed. "A bit closer. Good." His big hand wrapped around both of us and stroked together.

I put an arm around Gunner and gripped his back so hard that I felt my nails sink into his flesh. He growled—an actual animalistic growl—and seized forward to bite my neck. I cried out again, bucked into his hold, and was spending before I could find words of warning.

Gunner let up on my neck. "Harder."

"Wh-what?"

"Your hands."

I nearly asked for clarification again, because I was awash in total bliss and Gunner's request was simply *not* translating, until I realized I was still digging my fingers into his back.

Harder.

*Rougher.*

I sat up, throwing him off-balance just enough that I was able to push Gunner onto his back. I climbed onto his hips, slid my softening erection against his, and then dug my fingers into his chest. Gunner gasped and shuddered in arousal. He reached down and stroked us together again. I leaned over and bit his neck like he had mine, and that made him tighten his hold almost painfully. Then jets of warm release erupted between our bellies.

I let up on the soft skin of his neck and saw I'd left a dark purple spot. I raised my hands and could make out red crescents partially obscured by Gunner's chest hair. "I'm sorry," I said, glancing up. "I left—what? Why're you laughing?"

Gunner put his wet, sticky hand on my thigh and stroked. He looked sated—*boneless*—with a playful sort of smile on his face. "Don't apologize, dear. That's what I asked for, isn't it?"

I timidly set a hand on his chest again and petted once or twice. "Looks painful."

He let out a contented sigh as he sat up. Gunner took my chin and said, "It'll remind me of you." He nudged me, got off the bed, and walked across the room to the bathing basin in the far corner.

I studied him from behind as he washed his hands and then his prick. "Gunner?"

"Hmm."

"About Ferguson…."

He didn't rise to the conversation starter. Gunner fetched a new washcloth from the neatly folded pile on the shelf below the bowl, poured water from the pitcher over it, then returned to the bed. He took my face and gently turned it so he could clean the back of my head. I'd all but forgotten the cut, what with the explosion and running and… well, aftermath. I winced but remained silent as Gunner finished. He took my hands after, gently but thoroughly cleaning between each finger from when I'd bled at the canyon. Gunner lastly wiped my stomach and flaccid member before returning the cloth to the basin.

"I had the shot," he said, walking toward the pile of clothes near the door. Gunner glanced at me. "I owe you an apology for not taking it." He crouched to retrieve his waistcoat.

"Does Ferguson know your name?"

Gunner looked at me again as he stood straight. "You're very hung up on that one piece of information, aren't you?"

"No. I mean—if he did—I'd understand." I rolled my eyes at the absurdity of my own words. "Not, understand *that*. With *him*. But a history between the two of you and you are… human. Is what I meant to say."

"He doesn't know."

"Oh."

"Every man has a past."

"Of course."

"And every man has made at least one mistake that haunts him," he continued, removing the pocket watch. "It changes who he is. Sometimes entirely." Gunner returned to the bed and sat beside me.

"He's your mistake?" I asked, my voice low.

Gunner offered me the timepiece. "I'm his," he corrected. "You said yesterday it didn't seem as if I had the element of surprise on Ferguson."

I accepted the watch but didn't break eye contact. "Correct."

"Who in Tombstone would have known I was coming to Shallow Grave?"

"I couldn't say."

"No one. No one but Ferguson." Gunner glanced down and tapped the watch. "He gave this to me."

I finally looked at the watch. Elgin—and solid gold, if the weight was anything to judge by. I wanted to imagine Gunner kept it because of its practicality, but who was I kidding? It was a costly gift presented to a lover, and my holding it was about as wanted as a cart with a third wheel. "It's, um… very nice quality."

"I suspect he's using it to track my whereabouts."

I fumbled, then snagged the chain before the watch

would have dropped to the floor. "What? *How*?"

"He's a gifted engineer, Gillian. A little tinkering with the inner mechanics is nothing for him. And it explains how he wasn't caught off guard in the canyon either." Gunner stood, still naked and still beautiful. He walked to the window, turned, leaned against the wall, and studied the town below.

"Ferguson is afraid of you," I said, and when Gunner didn't reply, I pressed on. "He wants to know your location because he can't kill you."

Gunner raised one dark brow.

"They say you're unkillable," I replied to that singular change in his expression.

"Do they?" There was no particular inflection in his tone.

"If Ferguson can't beat you, he means to always remain one step ahead of you," I concluded. "The silver to counteract your Waterbury. Tracking you." I held up the pocket watch to stress my point. "Will you tell me why?"

"It's not relevant."

*Of course not.*

It'd been a tumble between the sheets with us. That was all. We were not friends, for God's sake. Gunner owed me nothing. No details of his past. No explanation of his relationship with Ferguson. No reason to see me again after—

"I think I know how we can find him," Gunner

said quietly. He was studying the sky now. "And end this once and for all."

# VII

*October 11, 1881*

"Are you certain about this?"

"It'll be like ringing the chuckwagon bell."

I pushed my suit coat back and settled one hand on a hip. "That's not what I meant."

"I know what you meant." Gunner set the gold pocket watch down in the middle of the street outside Bassett Lodge. He returned to my side and loaded a single nonmagic bullet into his Waterbury. Without another word, he cocked the pistol, turned, took aim, and fired. The watch shattered into a hundred little gizmo pieces. Gunner holstered the weapon before the shot even had a chance to echo down the dark, empty street.

I passed him the bundle of rope I'd held in my other hand. "You should come to New York."

Gunner took the end of the rope, dropped the rest,

and began looping a knot. "Should I?" he asked, not looking at me.

"That is—if you're in the area. I wouldn't mind seeing you again. *Privately*, of course. No reason to bring badges into this."

Gunner pulled one knot through a second and then reached for the other end of the rope. "You're not wearing yours," he answered absently.

I glanced down at the tear in my waistcoat, then up at him. "No. Ferguson flung it somewhere."

After a final loop, Gunner had a lasso in his hands. "I don't go up North." He met my gaze stoically.

I smiled, but it crumbled like ash in a light breeze. "I don't know why I said it."

"Gillian."

"Too much law and order," I said for him.

Gunner still hadn't looked away. Those blue eyes were diving right into my soul again, only this time, the darkness was clear as day and—*hell*. Desire? Need? Affection? Whatever emotion I was grappling with, the tangled mess inside me was entirely too visible and he saw more than he should have.

"You deserve better," he said flatly. "Not a man whose likeness resides in the rogues' gallery."

"Men like us—"

Gunner reached out and lightly stroked the gray on the side of my head. What I fondly thought to myself as a wing of Hermes. "Some do," he said over my protest. "*You* will."

There was no better man.

Only Gunner.

Gentle, charming, wicked, and courageous *Gunner the Deadly*.

It was I who hadn't deserved his consideration. An officer of the law I might have been, but I was also a selfish and lonely coward to ask of him what I just did.

A *thrum* broke the stillness of the night. Overhead, blotting out the stars—so many stars, like salt spilled across Heaven's threshold—came the shape of a massive airship. The blimp sliced through the sky, the steam engine on its stern *chug*, *chug*, *chugg*ing along. A massive Gatling gun with two ten-barrels hung from the hull, and attached to either side of the ship, like the locomotive, were mechanical arms and poseable claws.

Gunner rolled his shoulders once, gathered the rope, and said, "Hang on tight."

I shook my head and muttered under my breath, "I swear, if you drop us…." I put my arms around Gunner's neck.

"Where's your sense of adventure, my dear?"

"I must have left it in New York."

I felt Gunner's laugh against my own chest more than I could hear it over the ship coming in fast and low. He raised the lasso and swung the loop in the air several times, waiting as the starboard arm extended and reached downward. Gunner let the rope go, secured it over one of the arm joints on the first try, and then we were whisked off our feet.

The airship took to the stars again, and we swung wildly from the arm. Steam roared and cogs spun as the apparatus lifted up, ducked under the blimp, and dangled us over the deck of the ship. I let go of Gunner at that point, kept one hand palm down, and caught the magic in the wind to slow my descent. I landed on my feet, looked up, and held a hand out to ease Gunner's drop.

He hit the deck crouched on one knee, quickly stood, pulled his Waterbury, and pointed it into the dimness. "You got my message," he stated casually.

I watched Ferguson slowly emerge from the shadows cast by the blimp. It appeared he'd given up the steam glove with remote access, which told me there weren't going to be aether canisters fired at us from every angle. Ferguson instead held a massive net gun in both hands and had a pistol holstered on his hip. But it was the pistol that immediately set me on edge.

I wasn't familiar with the origins—it was a bit larger than Gunner's weapon, brass, and four barrels. The only firearms that had been fabricated to shoot magic ammunition were the Waterbury pistol and Jordan rifle. That being said, I didn't believe for one minute that an engineer who had at his disposal Gatling spiders, a wall-climbing locomotive, and a goddamn private airship was going to apply black gunpowder and lead to his current situation.

"Gunner," Ferguson said, sounding thoroughly amused. "You finally figured it out, you sentimental bastard."

"This is your only chance to surrender to Agent Hamilton before I take you out myself," Gunner replied.

Ferguson's wicked grin encompassed his entire face. "I don't think so."

"Three," Gunner stated.

"You should have stopped me before Baltimore."

"Two."

Ferguson cocked the net gun. "I'm going to make you suffer."

"One."

"The same way that Danny did."

And then they both fired.

The kickback of the net gun was powerful, even for a man of Ferguson's stature. In fact, it nearly saved his life by deflecting two of the Waterbury's aether bullets. The third, however, hit him square in the chest, and I felt my own magic attack his lifeforce. At the same time, a heavy, intricately woven rope ensnared Gunner and he dropped the Waterbury. The weights crossed around his back, thoroughly tangling and throwing him to the deck.

Ferguson roared in pain as he dropped the net gun.

He put a hand to his chest, and I swear I heard the distinct squish of torn flesh and blood. With his other hand, Ferguson took the pistol from his hip, raised it above his head, and shot.

There was a crack of four bullets, but the sizzle of heat that wormed its way up my spine warned it was anything *but* regular bullets. Jagged coils of artificial magic followed the trajectory upward, and then it exploded—a fire spell.

*Not possible.*

Christ Almighty, this was *not* possible. The Bureau only employed the very best of the magic community, and all of our architects swore the only illegal magic we had to protect against and control was aether. No other elements could be manipulated and stored within a tangible item—a bullet, for example—or utilized by a noncaster without them having a connection to the magic that encompassed the world.

And yet there it was.

*Fire.*

The artificial spell hit the blimp overhead, and flames immediately spread across the cotton lining. Hot steam began to escape through the ruptures and the airship listed to one side. I righted my footing and made for the helm, now visible in the light of the fire, but was stopped when Ferguson sidestepped and pointed those four barrels at me.

"If I'm going out," he gasped. "I'm taking the pig and pig-fucker with me." He pulled the trigger again.

Lightning bullets.

My warning was only a split second, just a whisper on the back of my neck. A bastardized version of that prickle my electricity caused right before I cast a spell. So I raised my hand and called the real deal. Billions of volts tore down from the sky and followed the motion of my hand as I pointed it at Ferguson. My lightning met his as it was released from the ammunition, and the two burst and shattered in a storm of sparks. Arcs of energy sporadically danced across the deck of the airship, and I heard Ferguson cry out—likely having made the very rookie mistake of staring directly at the center of the spell without protective goggles.

But my assumed victory was short-lived, as his spell began to twist and shudder, like an animal in death throes. His electricity doubled in size, wild and unmaintained without a caster, and then it all but swallowed mine without warning. His lightning engulfed my hands and ran up my arms, and I screamed from pain I'd never experienced in my twenty-nine complicated years of life. It was nothing like the magic hurt I knew and was trained for.

It was feral. Sadistic. *Vicious.*

All of the veins in my hands glowed bright and my skin was translucent.

Then I smelled smoke. Burned flesh.

As the light waned, my hands were left striped— red and raw, bloody, and quickly losing all sensation. I dropped to my knees, cradling my hands against my chest.

"*No*! Gillian!" Gunner shouted from my right. He was still fighting to escape the net.

Debris fell from overhead. The airship was starting to dive straight down.

Ferguson was coughing up blood and laughing like a goddamn monster.

I raised one shaking hand, my palm toward the blimp. I cast another wind spell, and the raw energy coming into my body, mixing with my lifeforce, and escaping as controlled magic rubbed against my exposed nerves in such a way that I was sobbing in agony as I tried to save our hides.

But the fires diminished and the airship slowed its fall, then I collapsed on my back, unable to feel my arms. The edges of my vision were going dark—with blood or inevitable unconsciousness, I wasn't certain.

Ferguson staggered over to me, his entire chest stained with blood. He let out a wet laugh and weakly pointed the pistol down at me. "Say good night."

"Good night." Gunner put the Waterbury to Ferguson's head and pulled the trigger.

**VIII**

*October 14, 1881*

It's funny, the extraordinary lengths the human body goes through to protect our mind after a series of horrific events. I remembered the airship on fire and the unavoidable crash that would have killed Gunner and me if I didn't do something. I also remembered my hands, burned and blistered and quite likely annihilated by manufactured magic gone haywire after being cast by a madman.

But then there was nothing. I had no sense of time—whether minutes or hours or days had passed—certainly no sense of place.

And the first impression my body registered as I came to was not anguish or death.

It was life.

The whistle and trill of a mockingbird. A dry desert breeze. A cool cloth on my forehead. The metallic *clink* of a woman's chatelaine.

I opened my eyes.

"Mr. Hamilton," a matronly woman said with a big smile. Her hair was pulled away from her face, and a white cap was pinned to her head.

"Agent," I corrected. My voice was terribly hoarse and croaked like a frog.

"He said you'd say that." She was still smiling as she lifted the cloth and patted the sides of my face until they were wet.

"Who did?"

"The gentleman who brought you in." My blank look must have been enough of a prompt. "You're in Tucson."

"Tucson," I repeated.

"That's right. St. Margaret Hospital in Tucson. I'm afraid you're a little worse for wear, but nothing Dr. Barrie wasn't able to patch right up."

At that I looked down. I still had arms, it seemed. In fact, my arms led all the way down to hands, and from there, fingers. Each one carefully wrapped in white gauze.

"I'll be damned," I whispered. Considering the circumstances, this was a surprising turn of events.

My nurse clucked her tongue at my words. "We've sent a telegram to New York City. To let the Bureau know of your whereabouts. We weren't certain what code to use on your PDD."

I looked at her once more. "Sorry?"

She frowned and wet my forehead again. "Poor dear. Are you feeling feverish?"

"No. I feel okay," I answered, and that was the truth. I must have been supplied medication. "Where—the man who brought me in—"

"Yes?"

"Tall? All in black?"

She nodded. "That's him. A very sweet man."

"He's all right, then? He wasn't in any distress?"

"Oh, heavens no. We'd have taken care of him if that were the case." She set the cloth aside, leaned over, and helped prop me up in bed. "He didn't stay. Said he had places to be—but left money to take care of you and instructions to reach your office and director." She patted my shoulder. "We've never met a magic special agent. Your sort don't come out West very often."

"No, I suppose not," I replied.

*Gunner left.*

He'd dropped me off at a hospital like a babe on the steps of a local church. He hadn't stayed to make sure I'd recovered. Hadn't stayed to even say goodbye.

*You deserve better.*

I swallowed hard and blinked several times. I looked around the area as the nurse collected her belongings to my left. A man was asleep in the bed against the opposite wall, across from me. I heard a few murmured conversations on either side, a cough, a soggy laugh, but the rest of the patients were hidden from view by the white curtains pulled taut between our beds. A second nurse strolled past, pushing a wheelchair with a man missing a leg.

"I'll be back soon with a meal for you, Agent Hamilton," the nurse stated. "In the meantime, your belongings are on the table."

I watched the white-clad woman leave, listening to the distant *schink, schink, schink* of her chatelaine before turning to my right. A small table was pushed underneath the open window beside me. Arranged neatly on top was my Personal Discussion Device, Gunner's pair of purple-tinted goggles, and surprisingly, my badge, holding down a slip of paper.

I reached a shaking hand out, fumbled a few times, then managed to drag the folded paper across the tabletop and pick it up. My fingers were stiff, sore, with almost no motor control to speak of, but I determinedly bent, tore, and crumpled the note until I got it open. It was a stamped receipt from Bartholomew Industries, the same airship company I'd traveled on to reach this god-awful territory.

The receipt contained ticket information—but not my own. One adult passenger. Dodge City, Kansas, to New York City, arrival at dock eleven on December 31, 1881.

At the bottom was a single handwritten request:

Meet me.

Yours,

Constantine G.

"Constantine," I whispered, and his name was like champagne bubbles on my tongue.

There was trouble afoot. Someone, somewhere, had managed to create the unthinkable—elemental ammunition. But for as disturbing as this intelligence was, I could hardly spare it more than a passing thought.

Because I would be ringing in the New Year with *him*.

With Gunner the Deadly.

Constantine.

*My* Constantine.

Gillian Hamilton and Gunner the Deadly return in the novel-length follow-up:

*The Gangster*
(Magic & Steam: Book Two)

Please continue reading for an exclusive sneak peek at the first two chapters of...

*The Gangster* (Magic & Steam: Book Two)

# I

*December 31, 1881*

"*Stop!*" I shouted as I gave chase to Fat Frank Fishback through the chaotic fray of Manhattan's Lower East Side.

Fishback—who was, in actuality, all arms and legs—skidded and slipped on the frozen cobblestones, righted himself, and made a sharp left toward a dilapidated tenement listing hard to one side. He shoved a big-boned woman from the open doorway and disappeared into the unsound structure.

"*Sonofa*—" I raced in the same direction, moved past the startled woman, and called a curt apology over my shoulder as I barged unwelcomed and unannounced through someone else's home.

The interior was dark, and despite the night of

winter already upon us, no lamps had been powered on. Steam piping had been installed throughout the Five Points earlier in the year, but it was obvious these people were too poor even for steam energy to light their home. The odds of finding an illegal syphon installed somewhere on the property in order to suck the teat of the city's steam grid were quite good. The installation in the slums had created a point of serious contention with government officials and the Old Money of New York City. Strongly worded letters had been published in the newspapers proclaiming it a waste of taxpayer dollars to light the streets of the wretched. As if these folks *chose* to live in squalor.

But despite the opposition, City Hall went forward with the investment. Funding had passed in January, and it became a matter of New York wishing to assert its dominance over other major metropolitans in the United States. The desire to proclaim itself superior to the likes of Boston or D.C. was a hell of a driving force. The mayor had used Grand Central Depot as his selling point—if tourists felt like they'd entered the city through the doors of a palace, then even the most unfortunate among us must have access to the latest advances in steam technology.

Access and means being two entirely different points, of course.

But I digress.

I wasn't here to chastise a too-full tenement of occupants barely earning enough to keep bread on the dinner table. I was here for Fishback. Nothing more.

I dodged the shadow of a resident coming out of a room, his curses now joining with the woman's—a symphony of fury and protests left unanswered in my wake. I raced along an extended narrow hall, shoved off the far wall in order to make the tight turn down a second dark passage, shot up a short flight of stairs, and finally caught sight of Fishback when he opened a door exiting onto a side alley, his rail-thin body briefly illuminated by the kaleidoscope of urban nightlights.

"Stop right now!" I hollered.

Fishback gave me a triumphant expression, stepped outside, and slammed the door shut.

I didn't slow my run, merely held an arm out, palm forward, and dipped into the ever-present elemental magic that encompassed Earth. The stream of raw energy churned and whipped at my request for its power, filled my body, and then erupted in a gale of wind. The *whoosh* of bitterly cold air blew the door off one rusted hinge and left it sagging like a broken wing. I ran outside, onto a set of rickety wooden stairs, hoisted myself over the banister, and jumped to the alley below.

I landed on the balls of my feet, shoes barely scratching a whisper from the cobblestones as magic aided me safely to the ground. But the door's now-unfortunate state had been what startled Fishback. He straightened from the bent-over position he'd been in and spun around to face me. His chest heaved as he fought for breath the winter air had stolen. Fishback's gaze flicked to the door and staircase behind me, and then his face blanched. His eyes grew wide. Panicked. Like a cornered animal ready to bite and scratch and claw until one of us was dead.

I had no illusions about my person. A man just shy of thirty, brown hair mottled with gray, a height and build hardly bigger than most women's, and no weapon on hand. So no, it wasn't my appearance that scared Fishback, a gangster known for squeezing the life out of coppers with his bare hands.

It was the technicality that I was *not* a copper. Special Agent Gillian Hamilton, active caster with the Federal Bureau of Magic and Steam, *thank you very much*. And it was my magic that had put the fear of God into Fishback.

"Fishback—" I started.

He turned on one heel and ran for the mouth of the alley.

"I said *stop*," I yelled. I tugged the brim of my bowler down and started running again. "Federal Bureau of Magic and Steam, Fishback. You're under—"

A glass bottle whizzed in front of me from the tenement on the left. I stumbled back a step to avoid being knocked out and turned my face away as it shattered against the outer wall of the building I'd just exited. Above me, the thrower shouted from an open window in a gravelly voice, "Magic pig in the alley!"

I broke into another sprint before a second bottle could hit its mark and slammed into the congested traffic of Baxter Street. All around me were unsupervised packs of children, stray dogs, wagons coming and going in either direction, and pushcarts *everywhere*, laws be damned, hawking the last of their oysters, knishes, and pickles before crowds dispersed for the evening. There were steam pipes crisscrossing building facades, rattling and pinging as residents powered on lamps and radiators. More metal tubing ran along the gutters of the streets, suppling steam energy to the yellow, red, and green streetlamps.

The voice from the window was still crying, "Magic pig! *Right there.*"

There'd been such volatile magic employed throughout the Great Rebellion that by the end of the war, Congress had enacted the Caster Regulation Act of 1865. On the surface, it aimed to bring the magic community out of hiding and make our intrinsic abilities legal to perform without fear of violence or jail time. But the finer details of the law required that every scholar—those who studied raw magic and documented the manmade spells—architect—the ones who fabricated the spells—and caster—those who performed the magic, such as myself—undergo mandatory documentation with the federal government. Keen and critical oversight of magic usage would protect soldiers and civilians alike from what happened during the war.

That's how the Federal Bureau of Magic and Steam was founded.

I'd come forward when I was eighteen and applied

to the regulation, but due to my atypical caster level, the Bureau jumped to offer me a job, a badge, and perhaps most importantly, respect. For the last decade, I had been doing my damnedest to represent the magic community, to educate citizens and eradicate detrimental old wives' tales, all while upholding law and order in the city.

It was, to say the least, an ongoing campaign.

I dodged between two pushcarts and stepped onto the road, only to be abruptly cut off as three men moved to stand in front of me. Fishback disappeared into the throng of people.

"Step aside," I ordered, pulling back the open lapels of my coats to show my badge.

They were all taller than me. Bulkier than me. With the sort of wicked smiles seen on men who used their fists to demand respect. The one on the left had his arms crossed over his barrel chest, with the stub of a smoking cigar clenched between his teeth. On the right was a man with a handlebar mustache and a badly set nose from a long-ago fight. In the middle was Tommy McCarthy, a known member of the Whyo gang that ran this neighborhood. He wore mechanical fighting gloves, the cogs spinning and pressure gauges releasing steam as he flexed his fingers.

"Look what we got here, boys," McCarthy said. He smiled widely, showing off a broken canine. "A copper on our streets."

"I'm not here for you, McCarthy."

"Know who I am, do you?" The steam whistled as he made a fist with one glove. "Scared, ain't ya?"

"No."

McCarthy blinked almost comically, glanced at Cigar Stub and Broken Nose, then tried to regain his footing by saying, "You *ought* to be."

"You're interfering with official matters pertaining to the Federal Bureau of Magic and Steam, and I *will* arrest you if you don't—"

"Arrest *me*?" McCarthy echoed with a bark of a laugh. "You ain't even tall enough to suck my cock," he replied, reaching down with one mechanical hand to cup himself through his trousers.

"I have no tolerance for your crude behavior. Step aside."

Broken Nose pushed back the folds of his coat and unholstered a Waterbury pistol. He pointed the three-barreled weapon at my head and cocked the hammer. "How about I put a few bullets through your brain instead?"

As the aether was galvanized, manufactured magic snapped and crackled in the air around me. A strong jolt shot up my spine and I shook it off. It was merely a physical response to the illegal spell reaching out to interact with my own magic. But seeing that Waterbury—

*An unkillable, deadeye marksman.*

*His finger pulling the trigger.*

*And blowing Milo Ferguson's head off.*

Those same fingers had held my chin just hours before while he whispered words that were seared into my bones like a cattle brand: *It'll remind me of you—*

*No.*

Thunder rumbled from overhead.

I raised a heavily scarred hand, palm looking as if it'd been used to press drying ferns, then snapped.

A bolt of lightning tore down from the sky and hit Broken Nose's pistol. The Waterbury exploded into a smoldering heap of scrap metal, and the ignited aether round knocked him off his feet like a horse had kicked him in the chest. The spark jumped to McCarthy's mechanical gloves—cogs and wheels flew every which way, pressure gauges went haywire, and steam valves burst. He dropped to his knees, screaming while tearing the gloves from his hands.

I looked at Cigar Stub, one hand still raised, electricity pulsating in my hold.

He stumbled backward several steps before fleeing without a care for either of his two-bit gangster friends.

I rolled my eyes and lowered my arm. The magic grated against the damaged nerves in my hand, and I shook it a few times to quickly dissipate the spell. Ignoring startled, wary, and gawking onlookers on the street, I carefully picked my way around McCarthy and Broken Nose, both groaning on the ground. I broke into a run in the direction I'd seen Fishback go and was surprised to find him within a minute. His form was hunkered down on the stoop of a shop shuttered for the night. A nearby streetlamp was blinking erratically, the red color pulsating like we'd been enveloped in the city's heartbeat.

Fishback raised his head at the sound of my steps. He shot up and started to run.

Finally having a clear shot of the man, I held my arm out and sent a violent gust of bitterly cold winter wind after Fishback. It threw him to the ground and kept him pinned to the cobblestones. I approached from behind while removing a pair of handcuffs from my coat pocket.

"I'll weep the day a man listens to me on the first command."


I hadn't pegged Frank Fishback to be a crier.

It took an astonishing amount of degradation of one's own morality to become known for having perfected the art of strangulation. For the New York police force to fear a single man. For the mothers and wives of coppers walking the beat to ward against evil when the name *Fishback* was uttered.

And yet, here he was.

*Crying.*

Fishback sat behind the bars of a cell on the fourth

floor of the New York field office at Twenty-Third and Fifth, where if he'd been on the north end of the building, he'd have had a beautiful view of Madison Square Park and Lady Liberty's dismembered right arm. Fishback's attire was still in a state of disarray from the arrest, and he had a shiner on his cheekbone from where I'd thrown him to the ground. But aside from those shuddering breaths and a wet nose he wiped on the back of his hand every few moments, Fishback had remained as silent as a mouse.

I stood in the narrow hallway opposite of the cells, window to my back where cold air leached through the old glass, staring at Fishback. I absently tapped the purple-tinted goggles hanging from my neck in beat to the *hiss* and *ping* of steam clanking through the building's heating system.

"How hard did you hit him?" Director Loren Moore asked in a thoughtful, almost curious tone. He stood to my left, as tall as an oak tree and built just as sturdy. He was over a decade my senior, with age-appropriate steel gray speckled into his ash-brown hair and well-groomed, if fashionably out-of-date, beard.

"I supplied ample warning to stop," I countered.

Moore lifted a pipe to his mouth, snapped his fingers over the bowl to light the tobacco with a flicker of fire magic, then took a few puffs. A heady cherry scent settled over us as Moore studied our guest. "Talk to us, Fishback."

Another quiet sob wracked Fishback's thin body. He shook his head while staring at the floor.

"You had a good thing going," Moore said, taking the pipe from between his teeth. "A real entrepreneur. Contracted by the Whyos to murder honest cops. How many counts, Hamilton?"

"Twelve, sir."

"*Twelve*," Moore said to Fishback. "Twelve times in two years you've pissed the police force off, and still they've not been able to organize themselves enough to touch a single hair on your head. So what happened?"

Fishback raised his head. He swallowed convulsively, his gaze darting back and forth between Moore and me.

"Was it the money?" Moore asked. "Is that why you started middle-manning the sales of magic ammunition? Not so smart, was it, Fishback? Because once word of magic involvement gets out on the streets, you become my problem." He made a gesture toward me. "And when I have a problem, I send for Agent Hamilton."

The compliment pooled in my belly and brought warmth to my cheeks. Loren Moore had been my director since the start. I'd spent years proving myself beneficial to the Bureau by taking on some of the worst backlogged cases that no other agent wanted to handle. My unrelenting hard work had been noticed—fairly early on, I think—but it had taken a few years before Moore began promoting me through the ranks. Now, I hadn't come into this career looking for an elevation in my status. I had just wanted to do some good. And while enforcing the law wouldn't minimize the skeletons in my closet any, it was a sort of... penance, if you will. And the relationship that had grown between myself and Loren Moore over the last several years was a bit like a weed sprouting between the cracks in cobblestones. Despite the odds, Moore trusted me, believed in me, respected me— and sometimes that was all that got me out of bed in the mornings.

I quite enjoyed Moore's company, and I do believe the same could be said for him, which was something, considering I am not the most likeable person. And while he *was* my superior, I truly believed that had I not worked under him, we might have been real friends. Although, when Moore praised me, I couldn't help but wonder if the weight of his words, the lingering silence in the moment, was wholly imagined, or if there was something unspoken he was hoping I'd pick up on. Moore was a bachelor, after all, but was he *confirmed*? Like me?

Huge tears poured down Fishback's cheeks, leaving streaks in the blood and dirt on his face.

"It rarely ends well when Hamilton returns to the office unhappy," Moore finished.

"It was for the money," Fishback blurted out. He looked at me, his breathing quickening. "Money. That's it. He said it was an easy job—that I'd make a hundred just by picking up a delivery and handing it off. A hundred dollars. *Shit*. The last mark I did for them Whyos was only fifty, and that was a hell of a lot more work."

"Yes, I imagine choking a man to death really works up a sweat," I replied, deadpan. "Where did the delivery originate?"

"Out West."

"That's over a million square miles, Fishback."

"I don't—California? Arizona? I ain't sure."

"Who hired you?" I tried.

Fishback gulped again. I feared he was one strong swallow away from taking his own tongue down his throat.

I took a few steps forward, wrapped a hand around one of the bars, and asked, "Would you rather a transfer to Sing Sing?"

"I wouldn't last the night, Mr. Hamilton," he protested.

"Agent."

"Wh-what?"

I expelled a huff. "Agent Hamilton."

"P-perhaps we can work out a deal, Agent Hamilton," Fishback suggested.

*Breaching my personal space.*

*Sweet and herbal breath whispering against my ear.*

*His cobalt eyes recognizing a tendency—sensing*

*a mutual attraction.*

I heard those spoken words, but they weren't in Fishback's voice. It was low. Smoky. Masculine.

Every *tick* of cogs, I thought of him, and every *tock* of second hands brought him closer. I felt as if I were a man with a mechanical heart and Gunner the Deadly held the winding key. I touched the breast of my suit coat with my free hand, where I carried the travel receipt from Bartholomew Industries in the pocket. The handwritten message at the bottom was simple. Only a few words. But the weight of them, as carefully chosen as when he decided to speak or let a moment linger on in silence, had changed everything.

*Meet me.*

*Yours,*

*Constantine G.*

The infamous all-black-wearing, gunslinging, criminal-killing, airship-robbing outlaw had trusted me—*a lawman*, for heaven's sake—with something sacred.

Something that perhaps no living person on God's green Earth knew.

His name.

*Constantine.*

"Hamilton?" Moore's voice penetrated the fog of distress and zeal that'd been consuming me since returning from Arizona territory.

I startled and glanced at Moore. "Sorry, sir."

I cleared my throat and turned to Fishback. "The only consideration I will make is holding you in our office overnight instead of an immediate transfer to Sing Sing. You've got this cell to yourself, a heated building, and"—I jutted a thumb at the window behind me—"perhaps you'll even catch a stray firework or two tonight."

"He'll find me here. *Kill me*," Fishback protested.

"Impossible," I answered. "This office is staffed around the clock. Our agents are some of the finest in the country, and we're on no one's books."

Fishback wiped his face on the sleeve of his coat.

"Who hired you?" I asked again.

"I ain't got his real name."

"Fishback—"

"It's the truth Mr.—ah, Agent Hamilton. I swear it. Only ever knew him as Tick Tock. New to the streets, but a true gangster if there ever was one. But I ain't even met the man. Only moved a handful of deliveries for him before you *intervened*."

Moore made a sound under his breath and another cloud of cherry smoke filled the hall.

I pushed my coats back and set my hands on my hips. "Why do you fear a man whom you've never met?"

Fishback stared at me like a dead man walking. "Tick Tock got an architect working for him, better than anyone in this building."

"I highly doubt—"

"Agent Hamilton," Fishback whispered. He was desperate. "I *know*. I middle-manned those crates myself. I met with a magical mechanical man who picked 'em up on Tick Tock's behalf. They weren't no aether bullets. They were fire."

# II

*December 31, 1881*

"The incidents are related."

"Take a seat, Hamilton."

I draped my winter coat over the back of a chair positioned in front of Moore's desk, sat, crossed my legs, and let my bowler rest on my knee. The private office was aglow with warm yellow bulbs. Outside the window behind Moore's desk were tendrils of light from a green streetlamp four stories down and a blue safety light atop our building to warn any illegal, low-flying airships in the night. The illumination met in the middle, catching falling snow in a medley of color.

Moore shut the door, hung his suit coat on the brass rack beside it, then moved around me. Still standing, he tapped ash from his pipe into a glass tray atop the desk. "We have no evidence that this Tick Tock character is directly, or even indirectly, related to your incident in Shallow Grave."

I sighed audibly.

"But," Moore continued, setting his pipe down, "your tone aside—"

His pause was enough to make me squirm.

"I do agree that the probability of two criminals simultaneously unlocking the secret to storing elemental magic in a tangible manner is not likely." He smiled, and there was an amused twinkle in his brown eyes.

"Yes, sir."

Moore turned and fetched a decanter from the shelf to the right of the window. "What's wrong, Hamilton?"

"I've lived a long life."

He pulled the stopper, poured a splash of amber liquid into two squat glasses, and offered one. "This'll help."

I thanked him as I reached out and accepted the crystal. Our fingers brushed in the exchange, and a single arc of electricity briefly joined us before snuffing out of existence in a plume of smoke. The sensation wasn't unpleasant, per se. It left a sort of drunk-just-under-the-surface feeling. Moore and I were each high-level casters, but thankfully not elemental opposites—fire and electricity, respectively. That sort of touch was still dangerous, though, and was meant to be avoided at all costs. Magics interacted with one another. There was no way of controlling an automatic function. It would be like asking a caster to simply stop breathing. That was why the Bureau paired us magically inclined with bruisers—agents who hadn't a single spell in their blood. It was why the new hires at our field office were given explicit instructions I'd heard repeated so many times, they'd long ago been memorized.

*Special Agent Gillian Hamilton works alone. This is a safety measure put into place, and we cannot stress this enough, as a precaution for you. Should you find yourself in a situation that includes distress to Hamilton's physical well-being, do not touch him. Contact Director Moore on your Personal Discussion Device. You can find his code on page two of your manual.*

That was one of the many reasons I was starving.

For Approval. Attention. Affection. I knew this about myself. Knew that in October, I was a skeleton—so deprived of human intimacy and all its subtle forms, I had been wasting away.

And then I had met Gunner.

Gunner had been impressed by me almost immediately. He'd approved of my abilities instead of shying away like everyone else, be them other agents or civilians. His attention had been flattering, thrilling. *God*, it had been almost terrifying, the way he'd studied me and picked up on such inconsequential details, such as the brand of my perfume. And the affection… the brush of his nose against mine, kisses so erotic that simply thinking of them took my breath away. And perhaps what had touched my neglected heart the most: the way he had cared for me while I was in a compromised state. Gunner had put me to bed and seen to my belongings, shown care to everything from my expensive Richmond Bros. shoes to the Everyday Man brand of my shirt cuffs.

I used to yearn for these moments with Moore— moments when he would pass me something and a thumb or finger would touch my own, or when he stepped a bit too close, perhaps even brushing my shoulder as he did. These moments were the catalyst in what, long ago, had me questioning the intentions of Moore's bachelorhood. But whether he was interested in men in the same manner as myself, or I was simply overthinking every minute action made by an older, attractive man, the point was, those shared seconds had been just enough to keep me alive over the years.

Hopeless for what I didn't deserve.

But shamelessly yearning anyway.

Until now.

Because that spark and smoke between us was nothing when compared to merely the way Gunner looked at me from across a room.

"Hamilton."

I hastily took a sip of the whiskey. Smooth and malty, with a hint of caramel on its way down.

"Excellent, thank you," I answered automatically.

"Dublin, twelve years. How're your hands?"

I glanced up. Moore had taken a seat. He watched me, smoothing his manicured beard with one hand. I looked at the glass in my hold. The crystal had caught the light of a nearby lamp and cast skittering prisms across the wooden floor. I switched hands and flexed the left absently. "It's nothing."

Milo Ferguson—Tinkerer—had very nearly blown my hands off in October. He'd utilized the first elemental bullet known to exist. The spell had gone haywire without a proper caster to control it, overpowered my own lightning magic, and absolutely torched my nerves from the inside out. A doctor in Tucson had performed what I considered a miracle and saved all ten fingers, but I hadn't dared admit to anyone that while I could feel the weight of the glass in my hand, I couldn't *feel* the glass.

"I wonder how stable that fire ammunition is," I said, putting an end to the silence. "Considering how volatile Ferguson's had been."

Moore hummed in acknowledgment. "The community feared this moment would come. Had any other agent gone to Shallow Grave, they wouldn't even be alive to investigate this."

I raised my brows.

"That's the truth and we both know it, Hamilton." Moore sipped his whiskey.

My cheeks flushed and I hoped he'd only think it

was the alcohol.

"For two months we haven't gotten a single scrap of intelligence about who in the country might be behind the construction of the bullets Ferguson had on his person," Moore said, in an almost thinking-out-loud sense.

"Correct."

"Until tonight."

"Which could mean any number of things," I answered.

"I think it means only one."

"That is?"

"The prototype has been perfected." Moore leaned back in his chair and rested the tumbler against his knee. "Why else would we go from merely the two rounds Ferguson fired to the anonymous report of Fishback seen hauling an entire *case*?"

"If only I'd found him before he was able to ditch the evidence...."

"Yes, well, that'd have been preferable," Moore replied, "but I'm still looking forward to hanging this over Inspector Byrnes's head."

"Are you intentionally picking fights with the police?"

"Allow me this pleasure, Hamilton," Moore said around a chuckle. He had an easy laugh and a handsome smile. "Watching Byrnes's face turn as red as a radish makes me feel young."

I turned the crystal glass in my hold. "I suspect Tick Tock intentionally hired Fishback to middle-man his incoming packages. Tick Tock is a new-to-me gangster, in a city already overrun with gangs. But Fishback's an established name who'd lend legitimacy to Tick Tock."

"Makes sense," Moore answered. "I'd also add that Tick Tock must be a local boy."

I furrowed my brow. "Why do you say that? The packages are coming from, and I quote, out West. Tick Tock could be from anywhere and merely looking to establish roots in a heavily populated area."

"This mysterious *architect* is from out West," Moore corrected. "Fishback has made a career out of killing coppers in New York, and yet, he isn't on the national wanted list. He's hardly even known upstate."

I raised my tumbler and asked before taking a sip, "Police department ego?"

"Byrnes would be the laughingstock of this country if the likes of Boston or Philadelphia knew he couldn't apprehend a single man. And yet that's exactly who Tick Tock hired—a man who the police cower from. I'm certain it was intentional."

"I suppose you have a point."

"I like that you don't pull your punches."

"I pull."

"Even with me?"

"Of course."

Moore set his glass aside and threaded his fingers together in his lap. "I wish you wouldn't."

A palpable silence settled between us, and the rest of the building came to life in the absence of our conversation. Steam *ping*, *ping*, *ping*ed in the piping. A scholar laughed in the bullpen down the hall from Moore's office. Someone else popped the cork on a bottle of champagne, no doubt dipping into holiday celebrations early. I shifted focus to watch the magic in the room, glittering tendrils ebbing and flowing like the tides of the East River. But when the fiddleheads reached Moore, they unfurled and burst as if he was a lighthouse and the magic an ocean storm.

Moore cleared his throat and opened a desk drawer.

My vision snapped back to the magic-free plane.

"This is for you," Moore said as he set a small brown-paper-wrapped package before me.

I set my glass aside. "What is it?"

"A gift for the new year."

I'd begun to push forward in my chair, but paused. "Sir?"

Moore picked up his tumbler again and motioned to the package with the other hand. "Just open it, Hamilton."

I obediently took the package into both hands, set it on my lap, and tore the paper free. I worked the lid off the box and revealed a pair of polished black and gold goggles in a style often favored by casters. I picked them up and found a stamp in the leather identifying their origin: Odyssey Magic Wares. Custom builds and premium quality. I looked at Moore.

He finished the whiskey in his glass before saying, "So you can retire that junk you've been wearing the last two months."

The junk in question was the pair of purple-tinted goggles Gunner had left behind at the hospital in Tucson. Not that I would have referred to them as junk. They might not have been a high-end custom build, but they got the job done, and most importantly, they were a gift. At least, I allowed myself to think of them as such. Gunner had a motive, a reason, a strategy for every action he took in life. Leaving them had been intentional—they had been for me. And I had worn them each and every day, from dawn 'til dusk, since my return home.

But then the reality of what Director Moore said—*a gift for the new year*—sank in. Was it typical of a supervisor to present a token to an employee? I suppose if it were a means of thanking me for a year's work, that wouldn't be... unreasonable. I *was* one of his top agents, and I *had* been with the Bureau for a decade, after all. (Never mind what had happened to me while in Arizona.) So it was probable that that was what Moore meant by the gift. Because to even consider the alternative, that this costly item was being offered with the same intentions as Gunner's, was wildly inappropriate, no matter what I sometimes thought of Moore.

"Oh," I managed around the heartbeat lodged in my throat. "I mean, this is really too much."

"Hamilton—"

"I can't possibly accept this."

"Yes, you can."

I looked at Moore once again. He sat at a sideways angle, his body relaxed but face tense, as if I'd been called into his office for disciplinary action and not whiskey and holiday presents.

"It's very thoughtful, sir, but I feel I've performed my duties the same as—"

Moore made a small gesture with one hand. "This has nothing to do with the job. It's from me to you. That's all."

*That's all.*

Was it, though?

*Yes.* Of course. My God. I'd been isolating myself from human companionship for so long that I could hardly react appropriately to the well-meant intentions of another who, in my own words, I should have liked to call a true friend. Perhaps Moore felt the same. And this was what friends did for each other. Granted, I second-guessed literally every action of men because those with our inclinations couldn't be up-front. We couldn't flirt publicly or begin traditional courtships. So how on Earth were we supposed to communicate?

I hadn't a clue.

Gunner was far better at it all than I. In every

aspect, up to and including spotting his opportunities for a tumble in bed. He'd said men like us recognized one another. That it was a survival instinct. Well, it'd taken Gunner undressing me with his eyes before I caught on to his interests mirroring those of my own, so I suppose that meant….

Moore was still staring at me.

*I'm fucked*, I thought. I couldn't figure this out. Did Moore mean something further by this gift, with a subtleness I was far too dense to pick up on, or was he simply being kind and was unwed because he'd long ago married his career?

"Thank you," I said quietly. "Ah, about Fishback—"

"He'll keep until morning. No, don't protest. It's New Year's Eve."

"I thought the papers had printed something along those lines…."

Moore smiled again and the tension in the air eased. At the mention, he dropped his hand onto the folded newspaper on his desktop. "Did you see the *Daily Cog*'s wedding announcements?"

I snorted before I could catch myself. "Sorry. No. I don't make it a habit to review the comings and goings of society."

"You ought to." Moore raised the paper and turned it so I could see the articles in question he'd left it open to. "Plenty of cases have been solved over the years because of a bit of newsprint."

"And so what's the case today?"

Moore turned the paper to himself to read the text aloud. "Only Son of Old Money Set to Wed New Money Beauty."

"Scandalous," I remarked blandly.

"Mr. and Mrs. Frederick Bligh Announce"—Moore kept reading—"New York, December 31, Henry Bligh, twenty-seven, the only surviving heir to the Bligh family fortune, is to marry the twenty-two-year-old daughter of Mr. and Mrs. William Olin of 635 West Thirty-Sixth Street in what is certain to be the affair that sets the stage for 1882."

"Bligh's getting married?" I pinched the bridge of my nose so I didn't roll my eyes in front of Moore.

Henry Bligh was a fellow special agent and caster—his magic a level two on his best days, compared to my level five—with the New York field office. He was very handsome, very blond, and very, very rich. He was also a son of a bitch if there ever was one.

"This is why you need to read the papers."

"Rest assured, my life remains unchanged, even knowing that Bligh's blushing bride-to-be is about to cause an uproar on Millionaire's Row. Were the Astors invited?"

Moore glanced at the article once more. "Invitations to the wedding of the New Year include such prominent guests as Colonel and Mrs. John Astor, the Widow Vanderbilt, and former President

Ulysses S. Grant."

"They'll have to sit Grant between the two just to keep the peace," I muttered.

Moore chuckled again and set the newspaper aside. "His wedding is going to bring attention to the Bureau in the coming weeks, Hamilton."

"Attention is nothing new for us."

"No, but an agent who's also a member of high society, and one getting married no less, is going to bring unwanted attention on our office—gossip, and the like. I request that you remain cordial with Bligh until after his honeymoon at the end of January and the papers find something new to discuss."

I couldn't very well tell my director what I really thought of Henry Bligh—that he was an insufferable and spoiled man, unbecoming of the badge he wore. I couldn't say that because Bligh only showed that side of himself to me. He came across as charming and witty with the rest of the staff, while painting all of them a picture of myself as a bootlicker. That I only managed to be held in such high regard by Moore because I'd relentlessly fussed over him for the better part of a decade and wormed my way into the position of senior agent.

Bligh was also the one to spearhead the rumors that I was an immoral cocksucker who belonged on the Bowery. That I was a whore only worth the pocket change a man had on-hand. For nearly three years, he'd been doing this—jokes and lies at my expense—

belittling my hard work and dedication to the Bureau while simultaneously undermining the basic respect I deserved.

Henry Bligh made a mockery of me.

And it broke my heart on the daily.

"Of course, sir," I said, the words ringing hollow in my ears. "If I may only say, I find it disconcerting that for a man preparing for what should be the happiest moment of his life, I hadn't even realized Bligh was courting. That's all."

Moore's expression was unbearably serious as he said simply, "Too many courtships these days are out of obligation, not love, Hamilton."

"Yes, sir."

With that, Moore poured himself a second glass of whiskey, motioned to myself, an offer I declined, then asked, "Do you have plans?"

"What's that?"

"For this evening."

Suddenly, the receipt in my breast pocket felt as if it were scorching right through my layers of clothing and Gunner's signature—*Constantine G.*—was branded to my flesh. "Yes." My God, did I imagine the corner of Moore's mouth turn down or was I projecting again? "A family friend is coming into the city for a visit," I added in a rush.

"Oh?" He seemed relieved. "From where?"

"Dodge City."

"Tomorrow, then?"

"Tonight," I corrected.

Moore's frown was back, but it was obvious and a little puzzled. He once again picked up the newspaper, unfolded it, and turned to the daily printout of the airship timetables. "Bartholomew Industries is the only airline out of Dodge City, isn't it?"

"Yes, why?"

"They've already landed."

I pulled my pocket watch from my waistcoat and studied the face. "They land at seven o'clock."

"Holiday schedule," Moore replied, tapping the paper with his index finger. "Airbright Passages and Ora Continental too—they've all been scheduled to arrive two hours early so the skies are clear for fireworks."

C.S. Poe is a Lambda Literary and two-time EPIC award finalist, and a FAPA award-winning author of gay mystery, romance, and speculative fiction.

She resides in New York City, but has also called Key West and Ibaraki, Japan, home in the past. She has an affinity for all things cute and colorful and a major weakness for toys. C.S. is an avid fan of coffee, reading, and cats. She's rescued two cats—Milo and Kasper do their best to distract her from work on a daily basis.

C.S. is an alumna of the School of Visual Arts.

Her debut novel, *The Mystery of Nevermore*, was published 2016.

cspoe.com

# ALSO BY C.S. POE

SERIES:
### Snow & Winter
*The Mystery of Nevermore*
*The Mystery of the Curiosities*
*The Mystery of the Moving Image*
*The Mystery of the Bones*

### Snow & Winter Collection
*Interlude*

### Magic & Steam
*The Engineer*
*The Gangster*

### A Lancaster Story
*Kneading You*
*Joy*
*Color of You*

### The Silver Screen
*Lights. Camera. Murder.*

### An Auden & O'Callaghan Mystery
(co-written with Gregory Ashe)
*A Friend in the Dark*
*A Friend in the Fire*

NOVELS:
*Southernmost Murder*

NOVELLAS:
*11:59*

SHORT STORIES:
*Love in 24 Frames*
*That Turtle Story*
*New Game, Start*
*Love, Marriage, and a Baby Carriage*
*Love Has No Expiration*

Visit cspoe.com for free slice-of-life codas, titles in audio, and available foreign translations.

Join C.S. Poe's mailing to stay updated on upcoming releases, sales, conventions, and more!
bit.ly/CSPoeNewsletter

Made in the USA
Las Vegas, NV
05 September 2021

29648289R00085